KING'S WENCH

A Star Original

KING'S WENCH

Charlotte Denis

A STAR BOOK

published by

W. H. ALLEN

A Star Book
Published in 1975
by W. H. Allen & Co. Ltd.
A division of Howard & Wyndham Ltd.
44, Hill Street, London W1X 8LB

Printed in Great Britain by
Richard Clay (The Chaucer Press), Ltd., Bungay, Suffolk

ISBN 0 352 39808–6

CONTENTS

TO
KING CHARLES II
Who Did Not Do All the Things
He Does in This Book
BUT
Who Probably Would
Have Enjoyed Doing Them
IF
He Had Thought of Them

CHAPTER I

THE QUEEN OF BANDYLEG LANE

London was on fire. The ancient city had been burning for five days, from Aldgate nearly to the Strand and from Moorfields down to the banks of the Thames. Explosions as rows of houses were blown up to create firebreaks counterpointed the roar of the flames. And the streets were a screaming jumble of refugees, dragging their possessions on hand-carts, crowding to the river-side, offering astronomical sums to boatmen to carry their goods and themselves somewhere, anywhere, just so it was to safety. By day, black smoke blotted the sun; by night, long tongues of flame – a painter's palette of hot, angry colours, red and orange and yellow – licked the late summer sky.

The Lord Mayor, a jelly of hysteria, had virtually collapsed, blubbering that nothing on earth could stamp out the inferno. But individual Londoners of every class were showing enormous courage. Despite the scorching dry wind from Europe – the 'Belgian wind' they called it – which blew steadily, sweeping the holocaust westward towards Westminster and Whitehall Palace where King Charles II lived, they fought on doggedly, planting explosives, digging among the blazing rubble, pulling doomed houses down with huge hooks fastened to long poles. Others passed leather buckets of water from man to man – or man to woman – for the women were fighting to save the city quite as valiantly as their menfolk. Pigeons, bewildered, fluttered low over the collapsing rooftops until, their feathers singed, they plunged to death. Dogs and cats and rats, many of which had sought shelter in cellars, ran howling from basement windows, their fur alight, eyes bulging maddened with pain.

In Halfpenny Close a row of wooden dwellings with lofty peaked gables and mullioned casements, built in the time of Henry VIII, was ablaze. The upper stories overhung the narrow street. A dozen men grasped a pole and cast its hook over a windowsill high above. 'Pull now, for Jesu sake,' shouted a tall dark fellow of about thirty-five, his face smeared with soot, his clothes punctured with dozens of tiny holes where sparks had landed and burned through the fine stuff he wore. The topmost room, spitting fire, teetered just over their heads. 'It's coming,' shouted a woman.

The dark man looked up, his thick sensuous lips grimacing as he assessed the danger. A younger, smaller man, somewhat resembling him, plucked at his sleeve. 'Back, brother, back for your life.' The woodwork cracked like a rattle of musket-fire above them. 'Right, Jamie,' he replied. 'Retreat it is.' The team lurched back as the building began to fall. But the dark one, lingering for a last glance upward, was caught as a heavy oak beam tottered and collapsed across the cobbles. He lay trapped with the smouldering timber across his chest. The narrow street was a nightmare of choking dust and flying splinters of wood, glass and red-hot metal.

The one he had called Jamie screamed, 'Charles Charles!'

An old woman seized his sleeve. 'Whoever he is, sir, he's a goner. Save yourself.'

'I can't. I can't. It's the – '

He pushed among the crowd, calling for someone to help him lift the beam. But all shrank from the flames. Then another figure burst through, elbowing, shoving: 'While you dither a man lies dying!' It was a girl of about seventeen, magnificently tall. In the strong wind her ragged clothes streamed from her slim athletic body. Her bare feet were black with soot.

'Polly,' an old man shouted. 'Polly Fitch. For God's sake – '

Hands reached out to restrain her. She brushed them aside and plunged among the rubble to reach the man. She bent down, grasped the oak beam and began to strain. He stared up at her from red-rimmed eyes.

'Od's fish, a wench, a doxy! And beddable, too!'

She felt the sweat trickle down her body, and muttered, 'Help, man, can't you? You're big enough! Press against it and help me!' He arched his powerful back upwards from the cobbles while Polly Fitch slowly eased the beam clear by a couple of precious inches.

'Thanks, mistress,' he said as he struggled free. Polly pulled him across a smoking mound of shattered wood and plaster. 'Out of this, and back to your labours.' He stared down into her stormy blue eyes. 'Faith, you'd give a man a rare battle in the bedchamber.'

Polly's voice was scornful: 'Here's London burning and you can't lift your mind higher than your own codpiece.'

'A deserved rebuke.' He reached into a leather bag slung over his shoulder and withdrew a gold coin. 'May I make amends?' She took the money and thrust it into her bosom. 'And your name?' Polly turned away. The street was still ablaze. He persisted. 'I heard them shout Polly – but Polly who? Polly what?'

At that instant, Jamie ran up to them, distraught. 'Thank God, brother, you're safe!'

'Were you frightened, James? For me or for yourself?' the dark man asked with a grin. Before the other could answer he glanced about swiftly. 'The wench, the wench. She's gone. Her name, her name? Polly something –? Oh, Jamie, you're a rare fool. Always were and always will be. God help England when your day comes!'

That night for the first time the Belgian wind eased. Over the nearly destroyed city lay a filthy miasma of smoke blended with the odours of oil-stores and tanneries. Although it was yet too soon for the people of London to assess all their losses, everyone knew that thousands of houses had been destroyed, that churches, warehouses and mansions had fallen, leaving only the jagged shells of their stone walls calcined with heat to mark where they once had stood, and that the great Cathedral of Saint Paul's was irretrievably ruined, its vast roof collapsed into its nave.

Just as hundreds of the City's most splendid structures were gone, so were miles of mean streets where the poor had lived, the beggars, the criminals and the vagrants who helped to swell the half-million population of England's ancient capital. But here and there, inexplicably, the wilful flames had spared a street or an alley. One of these was Bandyleg Lane, a narrow sordid passageway, not far from where the fetid waters of the little Fleet River flowed past the foot of Ludgate Hill to join the Thames.

Bandyleg Lane was scarcely three feet wide. An open sewer ran down its centre. Half-timbered houses leaned crazily towards each other, so nearly touching as to bar almost all light from the filthy runnel, even on the brightest days.

'The devil takes care of his own,' commented a bourgeois tallow-chandler on hearing that Bandyleg Lane had escaped. And he was right. For in all the City there was no more unsavoury alley. To say 'I come from Bandyleg Lane' was as much as to say 'I am a criminal.'

Its houses were at least two centuries old, and the cellars even older, some dating back to the days of the Normans – perhaps the wine stores of forgotten noblemen who came from France with William the Conqueror.

In one of these underground caverns, known as 'Granny Fitch's kitchen', a dozen or so rogues and vagabonds lounged beneath stone arches on benches and three-legged stools, drinking Granny Fitch's gin. The air was dank and chill; a fire glowed on a blackened hearth.

One man, heavy-set, his cheeks rough with stubble, thrust a beaker towards the foul old woman. 'Another go, Granny,' he shouted. She leered as she tilted the leather jack. 'That's four you owe, Whipt Ned,' she said, making a mark on a slate. 'Gin costs money.'

Whipt Ned grinned – a lop-sided, unexpectedly charming grin. 'I'm going forth tomorrow. There's plenty of fools along the King's Highway to feel pity for a poor seaman wounded in His Blessed Majesty's service against the Dutch.' There was a roar of derisive laughter. A voice cried, 'Wounded! And yet no scar!' Whipt Ned ignored the scoffers and leaned forward. 'But, Granny, I need a woman for this business. It always looks better when a penniless veteran of the wars goes a-begging with his hungry wife at his side.'

Will Fitch, the old woman's son and father to Polly, stepped over, his face still soot-blackened. 'London's full of morts, Whipt Ned. Find yourself one.'

'You know what wench I mean, Will. I want your girl. I want Polly. With a mort like her on the roads, a man could make his fortune.'

Granny Fitch cackled. 'Polly's not for the likes of you, Ned.' She glanced around the dark, smoky room. 'No, nor for any of you.' There was an explosion of guffaws. A wizened little creature wearing a ragged soldier's coat snarled from under a shadowy arch, 'And why not? Polly's no better than the rest of them.'

'Then try and get her, Mark Lampson. Just try!'

Somebody shouted, 'He has tried. We've all tried.'

'Besides, Ned,' said Will, 'what would a hot-tempered, saucy wench like my Poll want with a beggar?'

'No more beggar than yourself, Will Fitch,' the counterfeit seaman shot back. 'I'm as likely a lad for Poll as any ruffler or clapperdogeon in this ken, and well you know it.'

'But where can she be?' Will pondered. 'I left her in Halfpenny Close and there's death in the streets tonight.'

A slim, dark man, his long black cloak of good worsted and his high-crowned hat marking him out from the others, had been listening in puzzled silence. Now he turned to Mark Lampson, who sat on a stool beside him, 'Does no man here speak the King's English? What are all these – these clapperdogeons and morts and what not – of which they rant?' His voice was the voice of a gentleman.

Mark chuckled. 'Don't they speak the same tongue in Whitehall? What's the king's woman, my Lady Castlemaine, but a fancy mort for all her silks and jewels? A mort's a woman, and if she's a strolling mort, why then she takes to the highways to beg with her man.'

'And a clapperdogeon?'

Granny Fitch adopted a respectful, whining tone. 'Why, good sir, he's nought but a poor fellow who brings along his little child to wake the sympathy of the rich.'

'His child,' said Ned, 'or anybody's child. You would like to learn our cant, friend? Then listen. Miles Dobbler over there's a prigger, that's to say a horse-thief. I started out as a lad on the kynchen lay – a poor orphan, I told the gentry I was – and gleaned a few pickings of alms. When I grew older I learned from another of the kynchen coves how to earn a farthing or two as an angler, with a rod, a line and a hook that you cast through a bedroom window to hook down whatever may be, kerchiefs and bonnets and such. Will Fitch used to be a ruffler – didn't you, Will? – putting himself forth as an old soldier.'

'Kynchen coves, rufflers, priggers – nay, 'tis all Greek to me.'

'Long may it remain so,' growled Will Fitch, 'for your own good, stranger. In that way there's one cove you'll never have to meet.'

'And who might he be?'

'Why, the toppin' cove.' The room fell silent. 'That's Jack Ketch. The king's hangman. The man who puts his dainty ribbon about your neck, so.' He made an ugly gesture towards his throat, then let his head wobble to one side, his tongue protruding, 'And tops you, so.'

Will broke off his monologue to stare with sudden suspicion at the man in the worsted cloak. He walked over to him. 'Who be you? And what concern is it of yours how we come by our bread in Bandyleg Lane? Mark spoke to you of Whitehall.' He paused menacingly. 'Are you a spy come to interfere with the rights of honest men?'

The stranger rose, for a knife had appeared in Will Fitch's hand. Mark Lampson pulled himself to his feet and stood unevenly; his left leg was a full three inches shorter than his right. He laid a hand on Will's sleeve. 'Enough, Master Fitch. Put the pricker away. He's a friend of mine and no spy.'

Will pushed the small, ferret-faced Lampson aside, and the point of his dagger rested on the gentleman's breast.

'You can take my word.'

'Your word, Mark Lampson? And what gage is that to offer a man? London is riddled with spies as we all know. Spanish and Dutch and French Papists!'

The outsider, white-faced but calm, spoke softly. 'I am no foreigner, but a true-born Protestant Englishman.'

'There's many a Hollander speaks as well as you. And it is said in the streets that it was Dutch agents who started the fire.'

'Aye, enemies.' A growling chorus of rumbles rose. 'Or Catholics in the pay of the king's queen from Portugal.'

'Silence!' Granny Fitch shouted, her scratchy voice cracking. 'We may be rogues, but I'll have no treason talked in my kitchen. Son Will, put up your knife. Mark, so your friend be not of the watch, the rest is no matter.' She paused, her eyes narrowing. 'But what *do* you make here, so far from Westminster?'

The man opened his mouth to speak, but Mark raised his hand.

'He is not of the watch. We have business together, Granny Fitch.'

'Then finish your business,' said Will, reluctantly thrusting his dagger back into his belt, 'and be gone.'

Whipt Ned intervened, self-pityingly, 'Patience, friends. We all have business, and doubly hard to transact in these hard days with the plague barely spent and now our roofs come down upon our heads. I dare swear the gentleman is no spy and has no ill intent, and I can tell that he is about to prove it in the only way a true gentleman does when he is among the poor who must beg their bread.'

Taking the hint, the man in the worsted cloak threw a handful of coins on to the trestle before Granny Fitch. 'Fill their cups, mistress.'

'A health to our benefactor,' cried Mark Lampson. Candlelight glimmered on the grimy, unshaven faces. Beakers were raised and the toast drunk. 'And a health,' said Will Fitch stubbornly, 'unto His Majesty.' The stranger bowed, then lifted his own mug to his lips and replied, 'May he live a thousand years, eh, Mark?'

'Aye,' said Mark, 'a thousand years.'

There was the sound of bare feet running down the steps outside and the heavy oak door swung open. Polly Fitch stood on the worn stone landing, looking down at the firelit scene. Whipt Ned, who had now had more gin than was good for him, started towards her, made a deep, mocking bow, and then stood swaying slightly.

'Mistress Poll, I have just had the honour of asking your

father –'

Polly glanced at him amused.

'For my hand in marriage, Ned? And what of all your other wives? I'm sure there is one in Yarmouth, and a second in Southampton and a third in Bristol. As a true Christian woman, I cannot make you a fourth.'

Ned looked abashed. 'I want you for my mort, Poll. We could make a mountain of gold together.'

'Shut your mouth,' Will Fitch roared. 'I'll have no daughter of mine –'

Polly silenced him with a glance from those dark blue eyes. She made a striking figure as she stood there, despite her rags, almost regal, with her long legs part revealed, part concealed by the rents in her tattered skirt, her high, proud breasts, her dark hair hanging loose over her shoulders. She was like a goddess come to the cave of the crippled Vulcan.

'Thank you kindly, Ned. But I'll be no man's mort and no man's wife, either. Polly Fitch will not remain long in Bandy-leg Lane.'

The room echoed with jeers at Ned. He reddened. Through the swirling smoke from the hearth he stared at the girl, still standing just inside the door. Her height, her extraordinary beauty, her mocking smile – all seemed to separate her from the company in general and from him in particular.

He stumbled forward, his arms outstretched, with some confused notion of catching her around the waist, swinging her down off the step and into his arms. Hardly had he touched the torn fabric of her skirt and felt the warm firm curves beneath, than he was rocked by a stunning buffet on the side of his head. He crumpled to the grimy floor. Above him swam Polly's features. There was fury in her eyes.

'No man shall touch me, Whipt Ned, without I give him leave. No man at all. Do you understand?' He tried to stammer an apology. She jerked him to his feet, then held him at arm's length, examining him coldly. He stood before her like a frightened chastened child. The anger ebbed from her eyes and suddenly her palm was soft on his cheek.

'Poor Ned, poor canting beggarman. I'm truly sorry I struck

you.' He shook his head to clear it, mumbling, 'Nay, Poll, the fault was mine.' She ignored his words, but gently. 'There are many morts for you, Ned. You're no worse than these other twisted creatures here in my gran's kitchen. But there's a wildness comes over me when a man lays hand on me. I cannot explain why. So touch me not, none of you!'

She turned, then paused, 'I heard a toast as I came in. Whose health was drunk?' Will Fitch said, 'The king's, Poll. The Black Boy's. This gentleman –' he gestured towards the corner where the stranger had stood. But he was gone, and with him Mark Lampson.

Polly's ripe lips curved in a sour expression of scorn.

'The king! What good is a king when the town burns down? Oh, yes, I remember how grand he was, and smiling, when he rode through London for his crowning, looking down on his people from his great horse, with his officers beside him, all proud as peacocks. But he cares only for his own pleasures, let others starve who may.'

Will interposed. 'After those psalm-singing Cromwellites with their long faces – Colonel Pride and Praise-God Bare-Bones and the rest – the Black Boy has brought merriment back to England. The theatres, the brothels, the dancing at the Maypole!'

Polly perched herself on her gran's trestle, thrusting the black leather jack aside to make room. 'Aye, father, and they say one can see him any day in St James's with his hawks and his tennis and his women.'

Whipt Ned laughed, 'He begets brats on them like rabbits on rabbits. He must be a rare bull between the sheets.'

Gran Fitch sniggered. 'No bull. Do they not call him Old Rowley after the best stallion in his stables? Rowley's covered more mares than any dozen fourfoots in England!'

Polly poured a measure of gin into a pewter tankard and drank deeply, wiping her mouth afterwards with the back of her hand. Then she laughed.

'They only say it of Charles Stuart because he's the king. I'faith, there are doxies better served, I'd vow, in Bandyleg Lane than ever that sour-mouthed Barbara Castlemaine is.

Deny that His Majesty's a raging stallion and he'll put you in the Tower. Aye, and cut your head off like as if you were a chicken for the boiling.'

Will said, 'Nay, lass, he's a good man and he's our natural lord.'

'No natural lord of mine!'

'Besides,' shouted a tatterdemalion, pock-marked rogue. 'you'd lift your skirts for him, just like the rest of his women, Poll, if ever he asked.'

'If ever,' called a man, with a deep scar on his face, 'she could set her bare feet inside the Palace of Whitehall.'

Polly laughed good-naturedly at him, for, despite the scar, he had an easy, mocking smile. 'We live in changing times, Jem Hoskin. She that's in a bleak hovel one day may be on the stage of the king's theatre the next, and in Whitehall itself the day after.'

'You're a dreamer, Poll' her father remarked. 'Who's to raise you to the king's stage, much less to his palace?'

'Some day – you mark my word – I shall be an actress. I can read, you know, and write, too, which is more than anyone else in this hovel can do. I'll walk upon the stage and all the gallants down in the pit will hang their mouths wide open. I'll play the ladies of Master John Dryden, and of Will Shakespeare – Juliet and Viola and the Queen of France.'

'All hail, varlets, to the Queen of Bandyleg Lane,' Jem Hoskin shouted.

Polly leaped up on the trestle, standing high above the crowd, her bare feet apart, one hand on her hip and the other holding the tankard.

'Many a mort today's a queen by eventide!'

Gran Fitch looked up at her.

'If your highness is so very grand, then why don't you pay me for that gin? Or is it true what I've heard, that queens never carry anything so common as money?'

'Nay, I've enough to pay for my shot like the rest.' Poll reached into her bosom. 'Here's a golden coin the gentleman gave me that I pulled out from under a massy beam today. Aye, and he was wellborn for all he was dirty with smoke.' She displayed the coin for all to see.

'It's a guinea,' someone muttered in awe. 'A true golden guinea!'

'Give it me,' screeched the old woman, reaching up, clawing at the girl's dress.

Polly looked at it. 'A fine handsome thing, is it not?' Granny plucked again. 'Nay, Gran, you'll have it. But let me look a moment before it vanishes.' She studied the coin. She had never held one in her hand before. Then she turned it over. She stared at the face on the obverse side, strong, with a heavy nose, full lips and a determined chin. She studied it closely. Then she felt the blood drain from her cheeks, and for an instant swayed as her knees weakened.

For the king's head on the guinea was that of the soot-covered dark man she had rescued from death only a few hours before in Halfpenny Close.

CHAPTER II

A WHIFF OF TREASON

Charles II rose from the barber's chair by the window in his tapestried bedchamber. As the man left carrying bowls, razors and towels, Will Chiffinch entered. From his fingertips dangled a pair of soot-stained breeches and a smoke-streaked tunic. Charles planted himself on a stool and thrust one leg forward while the new young Gentleman of the Bedchamber, Bartelmy Ravenscroft, knelt to buckle his shoe. The king surveyed Chiffinch's features quizzically.

'What's wrong, Will? You've a face on you as long as a member of Parliament's.'

Chiffinch, the king's secretary, spy, private messenger and intimate servant, held up the garments.

'Ruined, sire, utterly ruined. There are holes burned – look you – here and here and here, as big as pennies.'

Charles chuckled. Bart tapped the toe of his shoe. He withdrew his foot and thrust the other forward. 'Will, you can't play with fire and not get singed. And that was a blaze big enough to burn a thousand Guy Fawkses. Thank God it's over.'

'But what of these things, my lord?'

'Throw them away. Or give them away.' He burst into laughter. 'You know, last night when I came back from the city I was as black as a sweep. But I went around to my Lady Castlemaine's lodgings and, in a fit of kindness, pleasured her thrice while I was still as begrimed as Beelzebub. She claimed I spoiled her night attire. And do you know what I said to her?'

Bart paused in his buckling to glance up at his master's face with affection and amusement.

'No? Well, Will, I told her that my grandsire, Henry IV of France, a born Protestant declared himself a Catholic because it was the only way to please his people. Otherwise he couldn't have ruled. Old Henry was a wise fellow. I told my lady what he said – that Paris was worth a Mass. If that were so, I said to her, then London is surely worth a silken bedgown. And now I say the same to you, Will. London is worth a pair of breeches.'

His merry eyes grew sombre. 'They tell me thirteen thousand houses are gone. I have ordered tents set up in Moorfields, and bread for the poor. Will, send these garments along. Some poor devil may be wearing rags even worse.'

Bart Ravenscroft rose.

'Thank you.' The king looked at him, the dark eyes softening. 'How old are you?'

'Twenty-one, please Your Majesty.'

'Twenty-one.' His face grew thoughtful. 'I was twenty-one, Bart, when they defeated me at Worcester. Forced me to fly like a criminal, hunted by my own people. Remind me to tell you one day how I escaped from Noll Cromwell, God damn him and all my father's murderers. You know, I hid in an oak tree and dressed as a rustic. And played the servant.'

'I had heard somewhat of it, sir.'

Charles loved to remember the tale. 'And rode with two gentlewomen as their man, so I did. And slept at foul inns. But od's fish, I'm such an ugly fellow they almost knew me. One fool even said, "He could be the king. But the king's taller. Nigh two yards high." Oh, I was clever, Bart, clever as a fox in the chase, getting downwind of the hounds. But perhaps what really saved me and delivered me to France was what Will Shakespeare called "the divinity that doth hedge a king". It was God's will that I should escape. And that I should return. Pray God I may never be sent on my travels again.'

'The people love you, sire.'

'Aye, most do.' Charles rose and Will Chiffinch handed him his plumed hat. Two spaniels were playing in a corner. The king bent over, tugging their silken ears gently. He knitted his brow. 'Will, have they found Sultana?'

'Not yet, please Your Majesty.'

Charles donned his hat and stared at himself in a mirror. 'I look more a pirate than a king.'

'Why, sire, it is a king you see,' said Bart. 'He who looks a king – and there can be but one – is he who wears the crown.'

'And if I should lose my crown, less a king?'

'No, my lord, for you are God's annointed.'

'But, perhaps – in that unhappy circumstance – a little more a pirate?'

Charles glanced out the window. Below him the Thames rolled silently seaward, filled with small sailing-craft, wherries, barges.

'Sultana was the best of the litter. And loyal, too. She would never have run off from me. Think you she would have left me, Will?'

'She was a faithful bitch.'

'And bitches never leave their masters,' mused Charles. 'Not so long as their food bowls be filled and their cushions placed just so before the fire. No, Sultana's another woman, like them all. And yet I love the soft little thing. Will, get your pen and ink-horn.'

Chiffinch turned to a high desk across the room.

'Write as I bid you and then put it out as a notice throughout Whitehall. Even as far as Charing Cross. Now, let me see.'

Charles bit his lip, pacing the room.

'Gone missing. A black dog between a greyhound and a spaniel. She was His Majesty's own dog and doubtless was stolen, for the dog was not born or bred in England, and would never forsake her master.'

'Is that all, my lord?'

'All? No. Write on, Will. Must the king not keep a dog?' He paused. Then, always delighted to jibe at those who plagued him for gifts and honours, he added, 'This dog's place, though better than some imagine, is the only place wherein no one offers to beg.'

Will glanced up questioningly. Charles caught his eye.

'Yes, Will. That's all. Post those words up where all men can see them. And come now, Bart, the dew is almost off the grass. Play me at tennis a space before the cares of state overwhelm me once more.'

He left the bedchamber and entered his private closet. As if on cue, his dozens of gorgeously enamelled clocks began simultaneously to chime the hour of six. He lingered a moment in front of a carved and gilded model of *Royal Charles*, the ship in which he had sailed home from exile. The walls were hung with paintings by Raphael, Titian and Holbein, the cabinets filled with rare crystal, jewelled goblets and delicate china. His eyes roved over them.

'Bart, is it not better to be a master of beauty than a master of men?'

'No, my lord, for a master of men is the master of the masters of beauty.'

The king studied the young courtier. 'He's shrewd,' he thought. 'This one may do me good service.'

But he was eager to scent the morning air, and Whitehall suddenly seemed stifling.

'Come, Bart.'

St James's Park smelled sweet and fresh. There was only the faintest overtone of acridity from the dispersing smoke that still shrouded the City. But eastward, in Drury Lane, the odour of disaster still clung heavily, although the Lane's fine houses had escaped the flames. Polly admired them as she passed. A leather strap around her neck supported a partly-filled tray which hung just below her breasts. Polly was crying her wares: 'Pies, hot pies. Come and buy, gentles. All hot, all hot-o!'

She sold two to a pair of sedan-chair bearers who chanced by, summoned to one of the mansions – that of the Earl of Craven, perhaps, the Earl of Anglesey or the Marquess of Argyll. The striding young Amazon had already sold most of her stock in the coffee houses of near-by Covent Garden.

'All hot, all hot-o.'

As she moved down the Lane towards the Strand, her fine, rounded haunches rolling gently, Whipt Ned followed, keeping well behind so that she would not know he was there. His eyes betrayed two emotions – the hunger of hopeless love, and tenderness, the kind of protectiveness an elder brother or a father might feel. Ned moved craftily from one doorway to the next, always keeping his goddess in sight and himself concealed.

Polly turned off Drury Lane, following a path that led across a field to Bridges Street. Now Ned guessed her destination. It was the Theatre Royal, built only three years before, upon the king's order. Normally, His Majesty's Company of Comedians performed here, but the playhouse had been closed for more than a year, ever since the onset of the Great Plague.

Polly walked along the building's side to the stage door. It stood open, and beyond she caught a tantalizing glimpse of mysterious wonders. Old Nick Farrow, the doorkeeper, was nowhere to be seen. She set her tray down on his little table just inside, and passed through a tangle of scenery, heaps of wicker baskets, cardboard crowns, wooden swords, suits of chain-mail made not of steel links but of painted string, discarded ruffs, a hobby-horse, a sceptre. All tawdry, yet with a strange raffish magic that made her itch to lift the sceptre and to set upon her head a diadem of false pearls.

At last she emerged on to the great stage itself. Daylight filtered down through the glazed cupola high over the main body of the house, the pit, with its steeply-raked rows of benches covered in green cloth. She advanced to the apron and looked slowly around. Just above the pit was a horse-shoe of boxes, then a second higher up, and above both, the gallery.

Chandeliers, now covered in dust-sheets, hung from the proscenium arch. She pictured them alight, with their hundreds of candles. Dust motes hovered in the air. As she walked, her heels – for she was wearing her only pair of shoes – clattered on the boards and echoed. Experimentally, she stamped. The sharp crack rose to the gallery, reverberated and returned to her.

She thought of Nell Gwyn, so recently one of Orange Moll's girls, selling China oranges to the playhouse gallants at an outrageous sixpence each. Then suddenly Nell had become a star, sharing the stage with handsome, imperious Charles Hart. A fine actor, thought Polly, and even more, the kind of man a girl must know if she wanted to succeed. For was he not Will Shakespeare's grand-nephew, and privy to all that went on in His Majesty's theatre? Polly had squeezed into the gallery to see Nell the first time she played. She sighed, remembering how beautiful the orange-girl had looked, acting Princess Cydaria in Dryden's first success, *The Indian Emperor*. And how compelling Hart had been as the Spanish conquistador, Cortés.

Nell's lines on meeting and falling in love with Cortés ran through Polly's head. She envisaged Hart standing before *her* – not Nell – resplendent in his silken costume. Cortés – or Hart – had just told her of the manner in which the conquistadors attempted to ensnare the hearts of the Indian maidens. She felt a sudden tug at her own heart which translated into a voice, hers, echoing through the empty theatre, repudiating her lover's arrogant masculinity:

> *Your gallants sure have little eloquence,*
> *Failing to move the soul, they court the sense:*
> *With pomp, and trains, and in a crowd they woo,*
> *When true felicity is in but two;*
> *But can such toys your women's passions move?*
> *This is but noise and tumult, 'tis not love!*

She could feel herself as Cydaria, melted by the flame of Cortés's virility, learning that he had loved before and that his dead mistress still filled his mind:

> *Ah happy beauty whosoe're thou art!*
> *Though dead thou keep'st possession of his heart;*
> *Thou mak'st me jealous to the last degree.*
> *And art my rival in his memory;*
> *Within his memory, ah, more than so,*
> *Thou liv'st and triumph'st o'er Cydaria too!*

A shout broke in from the back of the pit.

'Well said, Polly. Spoken like Mistress Gwyn herself!'

Her hands flew to her mouth in embarrassment. She could hear the uneven thumping of a wooden leg

'Don't fret, Poll. 'Tis only me. Old Nick.'

The imaginary robes of Cydaria fell away from her and she was once again only a girl from the mean dankness of Bandyleg Lane.

'I've saved you two hot pies, Nick.'

'Thankee, lass, thankee.' Nick clambered up on to the stage. 'I'm sharp set this morning.'

They walked together to the stage door. Nick paid her and bit into one of the pies. 'Mortal good that be, Poll.'

Polly sat on the edge of a wicker basket and swung her long legs.

'Nick, it's true, isn't it, what they say, that Master Hart saw Nell Gwyn selling oranges? And knew she'd be a great actress and trained her?'

'Aye, he did, but only after Nell made him the usual payment. In bed, lass.'

'Then she was no better than a whore!'

'And why not? Her mother owns a bawdy house to this day. Besides, how is she worse than the king's strumpet? You heard the rhyme one of the king's gentlemen wrote of Lady Castlemaine, did ye not?'

'No,' said Polly.

Old Nick leaned forward, his sharp eyes gleaming with amused malice.

> *Full forty men a day provided for the whore,*
> *Yet like a bitch she wags her tail for more.'*

'I think the king's sadly deceived.'

Nick brushed the crumbs from his jerkin and roared with laughter.

'Not he. Old Rowley knows what goes on, but he's not one to think ill of another for what he does himself.'

'He came here, often Nick? Before the plague?'

'Often enough.' The old man shook his head. 'But now the players are scattered, who knows where? Mistress Gwyn's in Oxford, I hear, selling victuals in the streets to keep alive. But she'll soon be back. Mr Hart says they all will.'

'Is he to open the theatre again?' Polly asked eagerly.

'In December. All bright new painted. And they'll be wanting fresh faces, to please the groundlings.'

Fresh faces! Polly wandered out into the sunlight of Bridges Street. She almost fell over Whipt Ned, who squatted beside the door. He tumbled sidewards. As he picked himself up, Polly laughed.

'Every time I see you, Ned, I knock you down.'

Ned dusted his worn breeches.

'You're a rare big mort, Poll.' He nodded towards the theatre. 'Still dreaming of playing the queen?'

Polly seized his arm and drew him over to a flat stone where porters sometimes rested their bundles.

'Ned, it's more than a dream. They're going to open again this winter. They'll need new faces, Nick says. Think you the king would help me to get the ear of Mr Hart?'

He stared at her.

'The king? Why should he?'

'Because,' Polly reminded him, 'it was him I saved, wasn't it? Who gave me the guinea.'

Ned replied logically. 'Then he's paid you for your services already. Why should he pay twice?'

She dismissed his masculine logic. 'I'll go to Whitehall, you'll see. I'll go and ask him.'

'They don't let folks like us into the palace.'

'Not into the privy chambers, no. But all the world can walk into the Stone Gallery and watch His Majesty stroll back and forth. He'll remember me.'

'More likely send you packing.'

But Polly wasn't listening.

'I'd go straight up to him and curtsey, like this.' She dropped a low sweeping reverence to the astonished Ned. 'And I'd say, "Your Majesty, I saved your life in the fire." '

Several passersby stopped to stare. Ned's face reddened.

'Nay, Poll, rise now.'

Poll's voice rang out through Bridges Street.

'Never, my gracious lord. Never until you grant my dearest wish.'

Open-mouthed, a fish pedlar stopped dead and stared at the nubile girl.

'I'll grant your dearest wish, lass,' he leered. 'What o'clock is tumbling time?'

Polly turned her flashing eyes upon him.

25

'Be off before I slap you across the face with one of your own herrings.'

The fish-hawker scuttled away, and Polly turned back to Ned.

'I'm for Whitehall. I'll *make* the king listen!

Polly and Ned worked their way down narrow King Street, the crowded thoroughfare which cut through the centre of the royal precincts, passing beneath its two Tudor gatehouses. Whitehall had grown haphazardly over many centuries, from the days when it sheltered monks, archbishops and cardinals through the time when Henry VIII seized it a century earlier, until recently, when the Black Boy's father, Charles I, enlarged and beautified it. The palace sprawled half a mile along the Thames. Peaked roofs jostled each other, hundreds of chimneys reached upwards in serried silhouettes against the sky.

There were homely exteriors of black and white half-timbering, acres of rosy Tudor brickwork and newer façades of smoothly-dressed white stone. The place was a rambling warren of council chambers, galleries, tennis courts, a herb garden, a tilting yard, a cockpit and private quarters not only for the royal family, but for the king's mistresses, his courtiers and his government ministers. There were two thousand rooms in all. Some were cramped and heavily panelled in Elizabethan linenfold. Others were large, airy and decorated in the French manner with painted ceilings and gilded mouldings.

And the palace was alive with people, from nobles in their silken doublets and plumed hats to poverty-stricken suitors almost as ragged as Polly and Ned. Whitehall was accessible to all who wanted to speak to the king, to advance a cause, even to watch him dine; over the banqueting hall hung a balcony open to any citizen who chose to lean on the railings and look down upon the sovereign and his guests. But halberdiers guarded the entrances, keeping a sharp eye on the throngs who passed in and out, for religious quarrels and foreign wars had turned London, like every other European capital, into a haunt of spies, plotters and assassins.

That morning, Charles's childless but loving and patient

Queen Catherine, the Portuguese beauty he had installed at Whitehall on the promise of an impressive dowry which included control of the bustling Moroccan port of Tangier, was preoccupied with the aftermath of the fire. She had watched as her husband and his brother, James, Duke of York, rode east to fight the flames. She had worried for several nights. Was he safe? When would he come back?

The disaster had brought to her a special, personal grief, for she, too, had heard the rumours that the fire had been started by Catholics viciously intent on burning the city to the ground. And Catherine was a loyal Catholic. Even though she was the queen, she could not fight rumour; no one in the England of the time could combat the savage bigotry which made of every Catholic, no matter how exalted his rank, a suspected spy and traitor.

What preoccupied Catherine in her quarters overlooking the river that morning was the human tragedy.

She thought of the homeless poor, the old, the sick, the hungry, those who had lost everything they owned in the fire. She knew that Charles would provide as generously as he could for all who had suffered. Despite his infidelity to her, he was a compassionate man. But there was one thing she could do to help at once.

She had ordered her ladies-in-waiting to gather together all their discarded cloaks, dresses, shoes, hose, underclothing, anything remotely wearable. Catherine had ransacked her own wardrobe, and it was surprisingly small. Four years after her marriage, her family, the Braganzas, had still not paid all her dowry; and Charles's treasury refused to grant Catherine her full allowance until they did. Most of her attendants were far more sumptuously clad than she.

Now she steeled herself to part with the gowns she had brought with her from Portugal, heavily embroidered and old-fashioned with swelling farthingales. Although they had excited so much scornful laughter from the smart ladies of her new husband's court, they held sentimental memories for her. Even more so did those which had been made since she met and fell in love with wayward Charles. But now others needed

27

them. They must go.

Catherine sat on a stool with her ladies around her, counting over the garments, repairing them, packing them. She sighed as she examined the dresses: the pretty pink English gown with the true lovers' knots of blue that she had worn at her wedding; the austere black velvet with lace cuffs in which she had been painted before her marriage, so that Charles could see what to expect. There were dresses made when she had so happily and over-optimistically been pregnant, each time hoping for an heir to the throne. They only served to bring back the bitter sorrow of her miscarriages. She now knew herself to be barren. Alone in her chamber – she was so very often alone – she sometimes choked back the sobs, especially when she learned that once again one of Charles's many mistresses had born yet another child to the man who should be father to her own.

Despite her lustrous hair and warm Mediterranean eyes, Catherine was a sombre figure: the court was still in mourning for the death of her mother, Donna Luiza, the Queen Mother of Portugal. Her clothes were dark. All the court ladies had been ordered to dress simply, to wear only the plainest of coiffures, and to forego beauty patches.

There was only one rebel in Whitehall, Barbara Villiers, Countess of Castlemaine. Deliberately flouting her royal mistress, she remained in the height of style. 'After all,' Barbara had been heard to say, 'what do I care for some dowdy old Portuguese woman far away? I feel no sorrow and shed no tears. So why this mummery of a pretended mourning?'

Night after night, like an island of brightness in a dark sea, Lady Castlemaine's long-windowed chambers over the Holbein Gate were aglow with candles and alive with the merry sound of fiddlers as guests danced corantos and old country jigs such as 'Cuckolds All Awry' which the king loved. Charles, with one side of his nature, disapproved. But yet he could not quite keep aloof from the bright sparks of the Castlemaine set. He sympathized with Catherine and understood her grief; but he sometimes attended Barbara's parties himself.

The king that morning, after his game of tennis with Bart Ravenscroft, took his usual stroll in the long Stone Gallery. As the velvet curtains parted and Charles entered, crowds pressed around him. He was unfailingly courteous, bending down from his great height to attend to the importunities of self-seekers and the complaints of the genuinely troubled. For Charles was possibly the most democratic sovereign England had ever had.

On this particular day, dozens of visitors sought to gain his ear, most wanting aid after the fire. One had lost his home, another his shop, a third his warehouse and goods. Charles listened to them all. Bart, keeping pace on one side, noted down the names of the supplicants. At his other elbow was the Earl of Kinnerton, a slim elegant man of waspish tongue.

In the midst of the milling crush, Charles caught sight of the aged Earl of Clarendon, his trusted adviser all through the days of exile, and ever since. He looked agitated as he approached the king. Clarendon had grown crusty and difficult. He detested and disapproved of Lady Castlemaine, and made no secret of it; this censoriousness often irritated Charles to the point of anger.

'Sir,' said Clarendon, clutching a scrap of paper, 'I found this outside Your Majesty's privy apartments.' He thrust the paper into the king's hand. 'I beg of you, sire, to walk warily. There is a whiff of treason here. The country's in no mood for secret Papists.'

'It never is,' Charles replied mildly. 'But who is the victim this time? The queen again? Or my brother?'

'Read it, my lord.'

Charles knitted his brow, then read aloud:

> *'Our sovereign lord no flame disdains*
> *Whether of London's or Castlemaine's.'*

He looked up. 'Not bad, my Lord of Clarendon. And true. But scarcely treason.'

'Read on,' Clarendon prompted grimly.

> *'But London's Protestant, we hope,*
> *While Barbara's secret flame's the Pope.'*

Bart Ravenscroft remained expressionless. Kinnerton concealed a smug smile.

Charles said, 'The first couplet's the better composed, in my opinion. As for the second, it seems a trifle lame. Moreover, my lady Castlemaine's religious inclinations are surely her own business.'

'And the king's,' Clarendon sputtered angrily. 'The manner in which Your Majesty's *maîtresse en titre* worships God is, in days such as these, unquestionably an affair of state.'

'Nay, my lord earl, an affair of mine surely, if of anyone's.'

'Your people, sire —'

'My people,' Charles interrupted, 'know that, while their king may often meddle with a lady's body, he has never yet been known to toy with her soul.'

He turned to the saturnine peer at his side.

'Your work, Kinnerton, I suppose? It bears your stamp.'

Kinnerton inclined his head in acknowledgement.

'My theatre opens this Christmas-tide. Why not try your hand at a play? Your talents are wasted in Whitehall.'

'As Your Majesty pleases,' Kinnerton bowed. He cast a sidelong glance at his sovereign. 'And for a subject? Something historic, I think. Perhaps the adventurous days when the Normans stormed in from France, toppled the English king and conquered the land.'

'William the Conqueror,' Charles replied, 'was an ancestor of mine, my lord of Kinnerton. Thus, you see, a man of Norman blood still sits on the English throne — and by consent of the people and of Parliament. May I suggest something lighter? Some tale of bawdry and cuckoldry? I shall be glad to provide you with any information on the subject you may need.'

The tiny circle grew suddenly quiet. It was clear that Charles had topped the earl, for the king was known to have bedded with Lady Kinnerton.

'Your Majesty,' said Kinnerton smoothly, 'is most gracious.' He backed away, then turned and was lost in the crowd.

Although Charles concealed it blithely, Kinnerton's barb had stung. Barbara had indeed declared herself a Catholic.

The court whispered that she had done so not because she cared one whit about the Church, but because her conversion gave her entrée to the queen's private chapel. Poor Catherine, he thought. Not only had he insisted that she accept Barbara as a lady of her bedchamber, but now his mistress even flaunted herself when the queen was at prayer. He sometimes wondered if the bad-tempered, avaricious Lady Castlemaine was worth all the trouble she caused. Then he smiled to himself. Under the coverlets, she undoubtedly was.

At the public entrance to the Stone Gallery stood Whipt Ned and Polly. Kinnerton swept by them on his way out. The earl gave Ned a careless shove as he passed towards the Privy Garden.

'Ned,' said Polly whose eyes were on the king a dozen yards away. ' 'Tis indeed the man I saved. Think you he'll remember?'

Ned did not reply. He was staring after the disappearing Kinnerton. When he looked around, Polly was half-way across the room. But the king, with Ravenscroft, had reached the velvet-hung entrance to the privy apartments.

'Sire,' Polly called out. 'Sire, if it please you –'

Charles did not hear her and, passing through the curtain, was lost to sight. But Polly was on his heels. She tried to thrust her way through the drapes when two yeomen of the guard stepped forward, crossing their halberds in front of her.

'No you don't, my girl.'

'But I meant no harm.' Polly was suddenly overawed. Courtiers stopped to stare at the beautiful ragged girl.

'Now be gone,' one of the yeomen said roughly. 'The king has no time for beggar maids.'

She was conscious of laughter and contemptuous stares.

'Popinjays!' She spat the word out. 'When next you see me in Whitehall, you'll bow as I pass.'

Now Ned was at her side.

'Come, Poll, you'll do yourself no good here – and mayhap even harm.'

He took her arm and steered her out into King Street. There

they paused in the sunshine. She planted her feet stubbornly, and refused to be pulled away.

'Come, lass,' Ned said again, 'we're not wanted here.'

'The king would have listened. He would!'

'Stand aside, my good people,' cried a tall young man, carrying a staff. 'Make way for her ladyship, the Countess of Castlemaine.'

Barbara Villiers approached, elegant, sharp-featured, her auburn hair superbly groomed. Kinnerton walked beside her. Polly stepped forward unabashedly, to hear their words.

'So you will come to my little masquerade, my dear Lord Kinnerton? His Majesty will be there,' said Lady Castlemaine.

'I doubt that he'll be enchanted to see me.'

She laughed. 'Nonsense. His Majesty always forgives a wit. As I do. The Pope my secret flame indeed! What a wicked jester you are!'

She tapped him lightly on the cheek with her glove: 'I shall see you then, tomorrow night but one.' Then she glided on.

Ned nudged Polly. 'That man!'

'What of him?'

'He was the one who came to your gran's kitchen with Mark Lampson. The one who drank a toast to His Majesty!'

He scratched his head.

'Now what would so fine a gentleman as that be doing in Bandyleg Lane?'

CHAPTER III

THE SECRET OF *FANCY ANNE*

It was evening. The wind had swept away the last cobwebs of smoke. Ruined London lay outspread, hushed beneath a twilight sky which hung apple-green above the gutted houses, the jagged walls and the blackened broken steeples. The hush was uncanny: no sound of horses' hooves clop-clopping, no jingling of spurs or slap of scabbards against leather breeches, no rumble of waggons. The City was still almost impassable, its streets clogged with charred wood and crumbled masonry.

Polly Fitch sat on a step under the arched stone entrance that led down to her grandmother's kitchen, watching a half-dozen ragged children at play. Hands joined, they danced in a ring. Their sweet quavering reedy voices echoed through the shabby emptiness.

> *London Bridge is broken down,*
> *Dance o'er it with my Lady Lea,*
> *London Bridge is broken down,*
> *With a gay lady.*

The bridge was not broken down, Polly reflected, but a few houses on it were completely destroyed by the flames. She heard footsteps hastening across the cobbles towards the end of Bandyleg Lane. The dusk was gathering.

> *How shall we build it up again?*
> *Build it up with silver and gold.*
> *Silver and gold will be stolen away . . .*

It was Whipt Ned. He paused, staring down the lane, searching. He saw Polly and beckoned to her. With a single flowing movement that audiences at the Theatre Royal were later to marvel at for its sheer animal grace, she rose from the step and started towards him. At the corner Ned gripped her arm.

'It's Mark Lampson,' he said in an undertone. 'Come, Poll.'

He led her through the ruins of what had once been a sizeable street, and into another alley. Then he raised his hand warningly.

The apple-green sky was turning a bruised purple-black. The voices of the children were faint and far away.

> Build it up with stone so strong,
> Dance o'er my Lady Lea,
> Huzza! 'twill last for ages long,
> With a gay lady.

They were in front of a tavern, The Three Graces, its leaded panes lit yellow from the candle-flames inside. Beyond its peaked gables, the walls of the Tower of London shone, a ghostly grey backdrop in the dark. Polly could scent the salty tang of the tidal Thames on the breeze.

'Is Mark –' Polly started, but Ned put his finger to his lips and pointed. The door swung open and Lampson's twisted silhouette showed sharp against the glow of the interior. They heard his voice.

'Your pardon, sir, but I dare not. I'll bear your secrets for you if there's gold enough to be got, but murder – that I dare not!'

He stepped out, the door swung to, and he stood hesitant and alone. By the flickering light that fell across his face from the tavern's windows, Polly and Ned could see his cheek muscles twitch nervously, his eyes blink rapidly in fear. As he started away, two men, their hats pulled low, emerged from The Three Graces, and caught up with him. Each took an elbow.

'Come now, my good fellow,' said one in cultured accents, 'not so fast. Let us consider the matter again. It need not be as you dread.'

The other spoke more roughly.

'You've blood on your hands already. I'd swear to it.'

Lampson's reply sounded tight, strangled with terror: 'No, no, not I. The toppin' cove –'

The pair gripped him more firmly, and half-carrying, half-dragging the poor misshapen body, hustled him away into the darkness towards the waterside.

'The Earl of Kinnerton,' Polly said. 'But the other, Ned – who is the other? Do you know him?'

'Aye, that I do. Gallopin' Jack, they call him. He murdered a woman once on Hounslow Heath for her pearls.'

'A highwayman?'

Ned nodded. 'And a devil!'

'Then come, Ned. We must learn what they're up to.'

Ned held back. He knew that he and Polly could put up a good fight against Kinnerton and little Lampson. But Galloping Jack was another matter entirely. 'Poll –'

Polly Fitch was already gone. Ned had no choice but to follow her, or show himself such a coward that he could never face her again.

They soon caught sight of the three, Lampson resisting, crying out in protest, as he was pushed and cuffed. Then they disappeared beyond the broken wall of a crumbling church. The river breeze sharpened. Poll and Ned followed the three on tiptoe. They were close behind them when they stopped in a patch of deep shadow.

Lampson shouted, 'No, I tell you, no!'

'Then,' Kinnerton replied softly, 'we must have assurance of your silence.'

'You have that, my lord. On my Bible oath.'

'Your Bible oath!' Galloping Jack scoffed.

There was the sound of scuffling, a grunt, Lampson's voice high, incoherent, a strangled cry. Then only footsteps, moving over the rough stones, growing fainter.

Polly and Ned took one cautious step forward, then another, and another. Holding their breath, they stopped at last. At their feet lay Mark Lampson. Blood made a black smear across his throat. Polly knelt and laid her ear against his chest. Ned looked down in frozen horror.

'The heart does not beat, Ned.' She rose. 'Christ have mercy on his poor perjured soul!'

Ned tugged at her arm. 'We must get away, Polly, before the watch finds him.'

Polly stood in absolute silence. Her eyes strained through the darkness; she tilted her head to one side, listening. 'Hush, Ned. You can still hear the villains' footsteps.'

'Enough, Poll,' Ned pleaded. 'This is nothing for us to meddle in.'

She put her hand on his arm. 'Ssh!' The murderers' footsteps were as faint in the distance as fingernails tapping on slate. They were almost lost in the sound of lapping water – the lapping of the Thames on the tide's turn.

'Towards the riverside,' Polly said. 'They took the path to the river.' She glanced sharply at Ned. 'Do I go alone?'

Ned shook his head. He was numb, terrified. But he stumbled after her through the darkness.

During the fire, many ships in the port of London had been towed into midstream to protect them from the flames. Others had been worked down-river beyond the inferno's reach. Several, inward-bound from foreign shores, had dropped anchor in the safety of the estuary. One of these, *Fancy Anne*, a small, three-masted, square-rigged vessel, had now moved up to the embankment near the Tower of London, and lay moored at one of the few wharves that had escaped the blaze. Her port of registry was Bristol, but a glance at her log would have shown that she had just completed a passage across the North Sea from Holland.

The Earl of Kinnerton and Galloping Jack crossed the waterfront and hailed a man whose outline appeared dimly above them on the deck. 'Ho, Captain Pargiter!'

The captain leaned over, peering down, a lantern in his hand.

'Is it you, my lord?'

Kinnerton broke in softly. 'No names, captain, if you please. Have you brought my merchandise from the Low Countries?'

'All safe and sound. Come aboard, gentlemen.'

Kinnerton and the highwayman climbed the ladder. Polly and Ned, from the shelter of a ruined warehouse, watched. Kinnerton's voice drawled insolently through the stillness.

'There's a mighty foul stink aboard your vessel, captain.'

The captain laughed.

'A drawback of the trade, sir. It cannot be avoided. But at least it's the stink of money. Will you follow me to the cabin?'

Kinnerton hesitated. 'Where's your crew? We're not likely to be surprised, are we?'

'No fear of that. They're all ashore boozing and wenching. This way, sirs, if you please.'

Their steps rang hollowly on the wooden deck as they walked aft and disappeared into the stern cabin.

Polly whispered, 'Merchandise from the Lowlands? What could he have meant by that?'

Ned shook his head slowly. 'It might be smuggling. Spanish wines and strong waters and that, from Flanders. Or Holland's gin.'

Polly's lip curled in disbelief. 'Does a Whitehall nobleman murder a poor wretch like Lampson for a few bottles of brandy? No, Ned, there's something else. Something more evil. Something Mark was too frightened to do.' She put her hand to her forehead, remembering. 'We did hear talk of killing, did we not?'

Whipt Ned nodded slowly. 'You've the right of it there, Poll. The toppin' cove. Mark spoke of him.'

'It's not a mere trifle like smuggling then, that's certain.'

Ned sniffed the air.

'That smell! Phew! It's horrid, ain't it, Poll? Even here, so far from the ship.'

'It's like the stench of animals. In a pen.'

'I think I've known it before in my life.' Ned pondered. 'Where?'

'Nay, lass, I'm no man to speak without being certain.'

'Then come,' Polly replied. 'We'll go aboard.'

'We'd be trapped if they saw us.'

'We'll not be seen. You heard the captain. The crew's on shore. They keep no watch.'

Ned shook his head admiringly. 'You're more a man than a mort, Poll.'

They crossed the cobbles and, with infinite care not to make a sound, slowly mounted the ladder up the ship's side. On the swaying deck, the smell was overpowering. A lantern, slung from the rigging above, swung in the wind. Its tiny flame threw dancing beams across the empty deck. The door to the cabin was tightly closed. They could hear voices inside, Jack's loud and aggressive, Kinnerton's quiet and authoritative. But it was impossible to make out their words.

'We'll do no good here,' Ned whispered. 'You get back on shore, lass. I've a fancy to go below.'

'On shore?' In the lantern-light Polly's face was indignant. 'Where you go, Ned, I go. It was I got you here in the first place.'

Ned knew that look; when Polly stuck out her chin in that stubborn way, there was nought to do but agree. He led her without another word to a half-open hatch. They descended the companionway.

A strange sight spread before them. The entire hold was bare from bulkhead to bulkhead, but along each side, half-way between the deck and the ceiling, stretched a wooden shelf some six feet deep. A single lantern hung from a beam. Polly crossed the hollow emptiness, then bent down. A little tangle of metal had caught her eye. She beckoned Ned over to her.

'Chains, Ned.' She whispered, pointing. 'Chains and manacles. Look, fastened to the deck the entire way along. There must be dozens.'

'There are, lass,' Ned replied. 'And if you look up upon those shelves, you'll find more.' He knew now what the stench was. Not animal but human. '*Fancy Anne*, Poll, is a slave ship.'

Polly Fitch stared. 'How do you know?'

'Because when I was a lad I sailed before the mast in one of these. To the shores of Guinea. Three hundred blacks we bore out of Africa that voyage, and sold every man and woman aboard in Barbados. We stowed them in layers, some on the deck, and the rest on shelves like these.' He glanced about. 'And manacled them in their places. We treated them like beasts, and you could smell our ship – slave ships always stink – as far as five miles off, if so be as you were downwind!'

Polly looked about the hold curiously. She had heard of the African trade, as it was called, but Africans were as remote to her as the Red Indians of North America, and their enslavement held no more meaning for her than it did for most English people at the time. She had never seen an African in the flesh – only pictures of them in broadsheets. Though of human form, they were, she believed, somehow less than human. Their nakedness, their black skins, their strange flat noses and gleaming eyes all conspired to distance them from her world. That they were bought and sold and maltreated did not stir in Polly, a kind and compassionate girl, the moral condemnation that would have been aroused if her own people – or even dogs, cats and horses – were brutalized this way.

Whipt Ned felt differently. 'A dirty trade,' he muttered. 'We'd be well rid of it.'

Strangely, in those early days of the traffic, when respectable men were making fortunes in a slaving company chartered by the king himself, there were few abolitionists among the educated or the religiously devout. It was all too remote. The full horror of slavery, which dawned slowly upon white consciences only with the slow passage of generations, was recognized at that time chiefly by the relative few who, like Ned, had seen it at first-hand.

'They must needs chain them so,' Polly mused aloud. 'Well, they be beasts, I suppose, and as dangerous as lions or tigers.'

'Not all of them, lass. Not all. Some day –'

He broke off as footsteps rang on the deck overhead. A hand holding a lantern appeared in the open hatch. Then Kinnerton peered down. Ned and Polly shrank back towards the bow, out of sight.

'All ready for our caged bird.' It was the captain's voice. 'As you see, my lord.'

'Very good, captain.' The earl sounded disinterested. 'Well, I must not linger.' The lantern was withdrawn, and Galloping Jack called out, 'Ready when you are, my lord.' Polly and Ned heard the earl and the highwayman descend the ladder to the wharf. Then Pargiter's rolling gait echoed as he walked aft. The cabin door slammed shut.

'Come,' whispered Ned. 'Now's our chance.'

They mounted to the empty deck and a moment later their shadows melted away among the vaster shadows of the shattered waterside buildings.

Shaken and bewildered, they worked their way through the rubble back to Bandyleg Lane. The ragged children were still playing their endless games and singing their endless songs. Now it was 'Oranges and Lemons.'

> *'Here comes a candle to light you to bed,*
> *Here comes a chopper to chop off your head.'*

As Polly and Ned descended the worn steps to Granny Fitch's kitchen, far off in a room in Whitehall overlooking the Thames, Charles II faced his eldest son, the Duke of Monmouth, a tall, richly-clad youth with a pale long face. The king's dark melancholy eyes surveyed him; there was love in the gaze, but weary patience as well. The lad's mouth was sullen, his eyes smouldered angrily.

Charles broke the long silence.

'So Jemmie, my poor boy, you would be a king?'

'Who has a better right?'

Charles rose from the chair in which he had been lounging and paced across the tapestry-hung room.

'By our constitution, you have no right at all. You are my first-born, that is true, but a son born out of wedlock may not succeed. Jemmie, my dear, I have done what a father can do. I have acknowledged you as my own. I have made you a duke.'

'But left me a bastard none the less.'

'You are what you are. It is a fact.'

'There are those who say you married my mother in France or in the Low Countries.'

'Married Lucy? Nay, that I never did, may her stormy soul rest in peace.'

'I've heard you even called her wife.'

'Of course I did. But in jest only, my boy.'

'And what if you have no heir by the queen?'

'I may yet have one. Catherine is young. I'm only thirty-six. And if I should not, then by law the crown passes to my brother. But you know all this.'

Monmouth's face showed scorn.

'Uncle James is a fool. Besides, it is said he's a Catholic – or means to become one. The people will never stand for that.'

'He will not change his faith if I can restrain him. But if he should – and I grant you, Jemmie, that would be a sore disability these days for an English king – he would still remain my heir.'

'You could legitimize me with the stroke of a pen, father.'

'How? By saying I married Lucy Walter? When I did not? I was in love with her – I was, I dare say, about your age then, and lonely. But poor Lucy was no wife for a royal Stuart, for the heir to the throne. Love soon waned on both our sides.'

The young duke felt a surge of furious resentment. Charles was so frank, so charming, so imperturbable, so utterly right. He made a last effort.

'Father, acknowledge me as your heir for now – at least until the queen bears you a royal son.'

'Never, Jemmie. I cannot by the rules of inheritance. And believe me, I would not if I could. You're not the stuff of which wise and temperate kings are made. You have a quick temper, a vicious streak and a petulance that stems from your mother's Welsh blood.' He seized both his son's hands. 'Content yourself with my love and my loyalty. But press me not for that which is not mine to give nor yours to receive.

He released the boy's hands and continued thoughtfully. 'Listen a moment, Jemmie. I want to tell you something. We Stuarts have a strange history. I won't go through it all – I'd be talking until cock-crow if I tried – but one thing you should now know.

'When my ancestor, Robert, came to the throne hundreds of years ago – the first of our family to rule – his eldest son, like you, was born out of wedlock. But later he married the child's mother. *As I did not do.*

'Even so, and although the Pope blessed the union and, by a special dispensation declared the boy the legal heir, there were many who insisted – and some who do to this hour – that our family came not rightfully to the throne. The skeleton rattles its old bones still, even in the palace of Whitehall. So you see,

Jemmie, the bend sinister has hung over us from the start, and threatened our claim to the throne.

'For me to try to legitimize you – a natural son, not a legal one, no matter how well-beloved – would be further to flaw our title. If you were ever to wear the crown, it could be snatched from your brows by the first ambitious usurper.

'Were that to happen, civil war would follow. And, mayhap, another Cromwell would arise to enslave our people and this time to end our ancient monarchy forever.'

'I would fight –'

Charles raised his hand. 'The English have had enough of fighting and dying in the cause of kings. I received a trust from my murdered father, Jemmie. Nothing in my life is more precious, not even your happiness.'

His dark eyes grew grave.

'Let me give you a warning. Meddle not in this matter of the succession any further. And do not listen to false friends who may try to tempt you with plots to unseat me and set you in my place. Angels have fallen through ambition. So may you, Jemmie, so may you.'

The king studied his son's face. Was there, he wondered, a flash of something approaching apprehensiveness in his expression, a flicker of uneasiness or of fear? Charles brushed the thought aside. His warning against the young duke's being drawn into any plot was no more than an arrow shot at random. He was sure that Jemmie would never harm him.

Yet London was filled with plotters. And Charles had many enemies. It was as well to alert the lad.

Lucy Walter had been prey to violent fits of Celtic romanticism during which any extravagant scheme seemed possible. Her heritage could be, for young Jemmie, a dangerous gift.

'You deny me justice, father,' the Duke of Monmouth insisted in a low voice. 'I am your flesh and blood, and so help me God, as I stand before you, I am the rightful Prince of Wales.'

Charles said nothing, only watched him calmly. Then the heavy mouth curved into a smile.

'Run along, Jemmie. I have work to do.'

Dismissed. Like a naughty child. Tears flushed into Jemmie's eyes; he turned and ran from the room so that his father might not see.

In Granny Fitch's kitchen Polly said, 'The king must know. Kinnerton is of his court, and –'

Ned interrupted, laying his rough hand on her strong brown one.

'Poll, those who bring ill tidings to kings often suffer for their effrontery.'

'I have a plan, Ned. This time I'll approach him in a different way. No stumbling like a beggar-maid into the Stone Gallery.'

'Then what?'

'I shall appear before the king as a woman. A beautiful woman. Am I not beautiful, Ned?'

A spasm of jealousy twisted like a cramp within him. But he only nodded numbly. She lowered her eyes until the long lashes stood out dark and fine against her cheeks. The ghost of a smile quivered at the corners of her mouth.

'Mayhap he'll not mislike me then.'

CHAPTER IV

PAVANE FOR A MURDERED QUEEN

Rain hissed against the long windows of Lady Castlemaine's
lodgings over the Holbein Gate in Whitehall. Below, Londoners hurrying home drew their cloaks around their faces and
lowered their heads against the wind. Streams of lantern-light
from the palace's many entrances glimmered on puddles
between the cobbles of King Street. By the gatehouse, sedan-
chairs waited, their bearers damp and irritable, while their
masters and mistresses attended the masquerade above.

For the first time since the Great Fire had broken out in
Pudding Lane, almost two weeks before, there was revelry
in the palace of Charles II. But this was the only sparkling
corner; in all the other chambers, mourning for the queen's
mother still reigned.

Barbara Castlemaine, her rich auburn hair shimmering in the
light of hundreds of candles, studied the scene critically. Like
her guests, she was masked and gowned as a personage of
another age – in her case as the Empress Theodora of Byzantium, in a rich, rustling flurry of heavy silks and Oriental
embroideries. But there was no mistaking the elegant figure
and arrogant poise of the woman who was still, after nearly half
a dozen years, the king's chief mistress.

Her influence was paramount within Whitehall. Many a
courtier had known the lash of her tongue. No English woman
since Elizabeth had excercised so much power, nor done so
with so careless cruelty. When she had insisted on forcing
herself upon the naive young Catherine of Braganza as one
of her ladies, the Earl of Clarendon, perhaps the wisest and
certainly the most experienced of the king's counsellors, had
been unable to protect the unhappy and affronted young
queen from her taunting presence.

To Clarendon's protests, Charles had replied sharply that
anyone who counted himself an enemy of Barbara's must

44

count the king his enemy as well. Clarendon still grumbled, but he did not press the issue; he knew his days at court were numbered and that Charles, though loth to cast him aside out of gratitude for his loyalty during the long exile, would sooner or later do so.

But Barbara was also treading the tightrope of royal displeasure. For a *maîtresse en titre* she had already lasted an unusually long time, even in the light of Charles's well-known reluctance to rid himself of any mistress.

'His Majesty,' a courtier had once commented, 'does not discard; he only adds to his hand.' Barbara felt certain she would never be wholly discarded; there were too many ties between her and Charles for that. She had born him five children, and he loved them all. She knew, what's more, that she still enchanted him physically: her very nymphomania – she had slept with many men in the court besides the king – lent a strange spice to their relationship. She was said to know all the positions of intercourse favoured by the ancients, and her scholarship in the art of love exceeded even Charles's own. Yet – and she knew this too – she had become a termagant.

Although she never hesitated if she chose to be unfaithful to Charles, she burst into uncontrolled fits of temper whenever he turned elsewhere. He had often berated her as a shrew, and once actually banished her from the court. But in less than a week, he was so hungry for her that he happily permitted the bonds of the old captivity once again to be riveted on him within the all-concealing curtains of the vast carved bed in the chamber above the dancing-room.

Nothing if not a realist, Barbara, her eyes cool behind the black velvet mask, stood awaiting His Majesty's arrival and casting up her sexual accounts. The debits almost balanced the credits. She studied herself in a long wall-mirror surrounded by gilt cupids that Charles had ordered for her from Louis XIV's *ébéniste* in Paris. The twenty-five year old woman who looked back at her was reassuring, the balance sheet still in her favour: the glint of diamonds in the shining hair, the soft demure lips, the deep decolletage that almost entirely revealed her breasts.

A servant tiptoed up. 'His Majesty, my lady.'

She turned, the double-doors were swung back and a major-domo called out 'His Majesty, the –' Charles appeared behind him, nudging his ribs. The man gulped and corrected himself: 'His Majesty, the Grand Cham of Tartary.'

There was a susurration of silk through the salon as the guests rose. Male heads bowed, ladies swept the deepest of curtseys, each hoping for a glance of special warmth from the slumbrous eyes gazing lazily through the mask that covered the best-known features in England. Barbara curtseyed lowest of all, and as she did so, one white breast sprang free of its bodice. A smile touched the king's mouth. 'Lo, empress,' he said in a voice only she could hear, 'I see the moon riseth in Byzantium, even on a rainy night.'

She blushed – it was one of the many gifts of this extra-ordinarily sensual woman – and readjusted her dress. 'Even Diana,' she replied, 'rises from her bed at the presence of so illustrious a guest.'

'Diana,' Charles observed drily, 'is not all that rises at such an encounter.'

He looked about the glittering room, returning the obeisances of his subjects. 'Your quarters are so luxurious,' he said to Barbara, 'that they remind me less of England than of the palace of my brother, Louis of France. Indeed I would think myself in the Louvre, were it not for your presence, Barbara. We can learn much from the French, but they choose their mistresses, it has always seemed to me, more as penance than as pleasure.'

'Does it please you to dance, sire?' He nodded. 'With you, my dear.' She glanced to the far end of the room where a score of fiddlers awaited her signal. Immediately the master of the music hastened over. He was a small man with dark skin and a monkey-wise little face. He held fiddle and bow in one hand and swept the king a deep and graceful bow.

'We wish to dance. Are the fiddlers prepared?'

'Indeed, my lady.'

She turned to Charles.

'What dance would you like, sire?'

'I dance only rarely,' he replied, 'and then badly.'

Barbara smiled patiently, recognizing a gambit her lovers sometimes used – false modesty. But even his hypocrisy charmed: he was probably the best dancer, as he was certainly the finest athlete, in Whitehall.

Charles went on, 'What would you suggest, *maestro*?'

The little musician's eyes twinkled. 'You have but to name it, sire, and I warrant you we'll know the music, every note. Will you have a pavane, a galliard or a bergomask?'

'Nay, they're all out of date. This is not the court of Queen Elizabeth.'

The monkey face wrinkled with amusement. He tapped the ends of his fingers with the tip of his bow, counting as he spoke.

'Then, my lady, what of allemande, gavotte, bourrée, passamezzo, passepied, rigadoon, saraband, passacaglia, cinque pace, branle? We can jig, give you a hey, a dump –'

Charles broke in, laughing: 'This is a veritable international menu of music. You start with the Spanish, proceed to the Italian and French and conclude with our own English country dances for a sweetener!'

'Or – I forgot, sire – a coranto, perhaps?' Charles nodded.

'A coranto let it be. To stir up my old blood. Three fast beats to the measure, runs it not so, *maestro*? With a last measure of six beats?'

'Your Majesty speaks like a musician.'

Charles shook his head, amused by the man's easy, cynical flattery.

'Not so, my friend. Between us there is only one musician and one king. And you are the music master. Let us hear your quality.'

The fiddler bowed and scurried away. Charles, stately in his long Chinese robe of emerald green, his jewelled belt and his plumed head-dress adorned with a single black pearl, led his graceful mistress on to the floor. Her ringed fingers rested lightly on his extended arm. The fiddles struck up a swift lively running melody, the king bowed to Barbara, she curtseyed and then with a sudden wild swoop – two lithe superb bodies flashing across the sparkling salon – the royal coranto began.

Gradually other couples joined the dance, protocol having been satisfied by the king's taking the floor first. Bart Ravenscroft watched thoughtfully. Although he was young and not long in Whitehall, he already knew much of the game – which duchess went to bed with which gentleman-in-waiting, who were Charles's loyal friends, who his covert enemies.

Bart was aware that, although Charles, since his restoration six years before, had won the hearts of most of his countrymen, there were still many disaffected about Whitehall – some who artfully concealed nostalgic Puritan memories of the days when Cromwell ruled as Lord Protector; some who cherished a revival of Scots Presbyterianism, the faith which had brought the king's father to the scaffold; some who hoped for an overthrow in favour of the Orange dynasty in Holland.

The Dutch, though closely allied by marriage to the Stuarts, were at war with England; many at home traitorously wanted the Netherlands to win. A Dutch victory, they thought, would spell the end to pro-Catholic sympathies in England. And an eventual union with Holland, with a Dutch monarch in Whitehall, would bring the French and, indeed, the Spanish as well to their knees. So long as Charles lived and ruled, his old friendship with France, forged at his birth through his French-born mother, would always hold within it the seed of a threat to Holland – and to Protestantism.

Bart surveyed the moving throng, so elegant, so rich, so ostensibly loyal to their king. Who were the loyalists, and who, in their hearts, the traitors?

His eye fell on the petulant young Duke of Monmouth, dancing with a slim girlish viscountess. There, Bart thought, dances an enigma in satin. It was no secret that Jemmie coveted the Principality of Wales and all it represented by way of inheritance. But ugly stories already clustered about Charles's first-born, stories of wild bouts of drunkenness, of outbursts of violence, of duels and even of murders in the darkened streets of the capital. A debauchee and a weakling, yet Charles adored him. Bart, unmarried and, for all his manly appearance still an unsophisticated boy, knew nothing of the strong ties of paternity, of the irrational love a father can hold for his son.

He studied the king, so strange a mixture of libertine and God's annointed. How well he kept the two sides separated! At the moment he was precisely what people called him, the Merry Monarch, dancing opposite Barbara, Countess of Castlemaine. They advanced and retreated, in a mock representation of courtship, skilful stylization of the mating of opposites. Each seemed wholly absorbed in the other, but Bart couldn't help wondering.

It was common knowledge that Charles had not visited Barbara's bed for at least ten days, and that he had been utterly besotted by the beautiful if empty-headed Frances Stuart – La Belle Stuart, one of the queen's young maids of honour, who had teased and spurned him mercilessly. Her recent elopement with the Duke of Richmond had, it was said – and Bart had seen Charles's strange savage moods of late – driven the king to bitter anger. Being denied by a woman was a rare and disconcerting experience for him.

'A maid's nay,' he often remarked, 'is nothing. It merely conceals the desire she feels but will not, at first encounter, show.'

Frances had deliberately led him on, encouraged at the beginning by, of all people, Barbara, who found the flirtation a convenient way to distract Charles's attention from one of her own affairs. But the girl had gone on with it, Bart suspected, for the sheer joyous bitchery of taunting the most powerful man in England. Now Frances was gone, banned by the king's order from the court. His Majesty would not readily find Lady Castlemaine sufficient compensation for his frustration, for the lightning in his loins which La Belle Stuart had roused, that darting flame which only its originator can slake and quiet.

The coranto ended. Lady Castlemaine led her partner to one of the windows overlooking King Street. Charles's forehead was damp with sweat. The room was warm. She said in an undertone, 'You will stay when the rest are gone, dear heart? Or perchance return later?' Charles looked into her eyes, his own veiled with speculation. What was coming next? 'You seem tired,' she went on 'Here would be gentleness, your brow soothed.'

Charles pulled the heavy curtains aside and glanced down towards the street. Two chair-bearers had just arrived, hooded against the rain. 'You have a late guest, Barbara.'

It was an evasion. She knew it. Best not press him too hard. The music began again. A pavane, slow and stately, in the Spanish manner. A groan of feigned dismay arose in the room. She signalled the fiddlers and once more the coranto began.

'You'll dance again?'

Charles shook his head. 'I must not stay late tonight. Od's fish, think you a king has naught to do but kick up his heels? In the morning I meet my advisers for the rebuilding of our poor city.'

His tone was harsh. She felt anger rise within her.

'Have you given thought, sire, to my new carriage and the four greys?'

'No,' Charles replied shortly. 'I have not. You know, Barbara, I do what I can for you. But my moneys are committed. You must bear with me in patience. And now, if you please –' As he turned, prepared to go, a footman approached.

'Your pardon, sire. Madame –' He paused waiting for her acknowledgement.

'Yes?' She was impatient at the interruption; she had wanted again to soften her tactics before Charles left.

'A lady has arrived. She will not give her name.'

'We welcome no strangers here. Send her away.'

'But she says,' the man hesitated and stammered, 'that she is acquainted with His Majesty.'

Barbara laughed, but the laugh was artificial, forced. 'Oh, Charles, another of your mysteries. But why was she not brought up the privy stairs to your chambers by Will Chiffinch, as usual?'

Charles shook his head.

'I expect no one.'

He looked interested though. 'With your permission, my

dear countess, accord her entrance.'

Barbara nodded, and the servant bowed and backed away. The sound of the coranto swelled, as the double-doors opened.

A magnificently tall woman, clothed in the blackest of black, took one step into the room, and then stood in majestic silence. Her dress was in the Elizabethan style, outmoded long since but superbly graceful, with its tight stomacher, high neck, white stiffened ruff and black net collar rising from behind and framing the superb head. She was adorned only with a cap of seed pearls, the centre pointed downward like a widow's peak.

Her mask, unlike those of the other revellers, covered her entire face. Through the eye-slits there were glints of deep icy blue. Nothing else which could have helped identify her was revealed. Yet the womanly magnetism hidden by the almost macabre disguise declared itself to Charles at once – the slim swaying body, the proud carriage, the utter self-assurance.

She remained motionless, an apparition. Barbara Castlemaine rose to her feet, ready to step forward and challenge her. But something stopped her. Perhaps it was the uncanny composure, the stark contrast between the stiff straight Elizabethan garment and the soft voluptuous femininity of the other women's gowns. It was as if a messenger of death had suddenly entered the warm, well-lighted ballroom.

One by one, the dancers halted, abashed by the newcomer's sombre dignity. Fiddle after fiddle fell silent, until the last notes faded away in broken measures, the music splintering on the heavy air like fragile glass.

Someone laughed, a nervous, hysterical laugh; then again there was only silence. In stately rhythm, the woman advanced towards the king, paused in front of him, and sank in the deepest of curtseys. As she bowed her head, he caught a glimpse of her bare neck. For an instant, he held his breath. What if the skin were marked, as he irrationally feared, by a thin line of red blood, as if where the headsman's axe had bitten? But the nape was smooth, young, kissed not by steel, as was the neck of the long-dead Queen Mary of Scotland, whose garb she imitated, but only by the sun of summer.

51

The king extended his hand. She took it wordlessly.

'Rise, madame. Will you dance a pavane with me?'

As the others fell back, the music began, deliberate and melancholy. Gone now was the feverish gaiety of the coranto. This was a dance of courtliness and constraint, with two beats only to the measure. The couple swayed with slow majesty, the majesty of peacocks advancing across the classic lawns of an Italian garden. Charles's Chinese robe swung to his motions; the stranger's high starched collar bobbed with gentle grace.

The dance ended. The hands of the pair fell to their sides. Barbara Castlemaine's self-control cracked. Her caution vanished, her nerves jangled. White-faced, she strode to the newcomer's side.

'How dare you?' she demanded. 'Whoever you are, how dare you come here to insult His Majesty so?' The woman remained silent, and Barbara blurted, 'To enter these rooms dressed as His Majesty's ancestor – his *murdered* ancestor! To mock Mary, Queen of Scotland! Have you no decency, no sense of what is fitting before your king?' She turned fiercely to Charles. 'Dismiss her, sire, or I shall have her scourged from Whitehall!'

His usually gentle voice whiplashed with anger. 'By God's body, madame, you try my patience! And why should she not dress as my great-grandmother if it pleases her?'

'I'll not have an image of death in my lodgings!'

He addressed the unknown guest.

'For what reason do you come in this manner? Mary was slaughtered by Elizabeth. Is this some jest?' His voice softened. 'Be not afraid, madame. To do this, you must have wanted to see me very greatly.'

Barbara was beside herself with fury. 'Forgive me, sire, but this foolery has gone far enough. You take advantage of His Majesty's good nature, madame. But you shall not take advantage of mine. I bid you to be gone.'

Ignoring Lady Castlemaine, the woman dropped a curtsey to the king, and then, rising, glided towards the door.

'Stay,' Charles called out. 'Stay!'

But the door had closed behind her. Bart Ravenscroft hurried to his master's side.

'Shall I pursue her, sire?'

'Nay. Nay, Bart. I am quite able to do that for myself.'

From the top of the stairs he caught a glimpse of her skirt disappearing into King Street. Gathering his full green robe up to his knees, he raced after her. The rain had stopped. Her chair-bearers stood ready to hand her into her sedan, but before they could do so, Charles had caught up with her.

'No you don't, madame. This way.'

He thrust aside two halberdiers who stood by an entrance into the Privy Garden and, seizing her arm, escorted her inside.

Rain had sweetened the odours of flowers and grass. Wind rustled through the trees. All at once the garden was flooded with moonlight, as the clouds were shredded apart.

They stood beside a sundial. He halted abruptly and swung the woman around to face him. The silver light from above glinted on the seed pearls of her cap. He reached for her mask and seized it. He was breathing hard as if he had just finished a game of tennis. A tension, an excitement, mounted within him such as he had not felt for almost twenty years, not since that night in the Hague when he had first set eyes on Lucy Walter.

He tore the mask loose. She made no effort to resist. It took him only an instant to recognize the face before him.

'I lost you once,' he murmured as he drew her towards him, 'but I shall not lose you a second time.' His fingers traced her features with delicate tenderness. Her lips parted as he touched them.

'It was Polly, was it not? Polly what?'

'Polly Fitch, so please Your Majesty.'

'It does please my majesty,' Charles murmured. 'It pleases my majesty most uncommonly, Polly.' As he led her across the garden towards the palace, the wind swept the clouds once more together, and the silvered leaves were dark again.

CHAPTER V

DAWN OVER WHITEHALL

Charles slept, but Polly Fitch lay awake in the huge bed. Although the night was cool, the curtains which normally were drawn around the ornately carved four-poster were looped back. A dying fire flickered fitfully on the hearth, casting outlandish shadows on the walls. In an adjoining room a clock struck musically, then others of Charles's clocks, all chiming together. But he scarcely stirred. He loved his clocks and often wound them himself. Their musical notes were part of the fabric of his life and never disturbed him; but many of his mistresses had been awakened by them from dreams of regal fantasy. As their bells ceased, there was a low whining from the corner where a spaniel turned in his sleep.

Polly's body ached, for Charles, though a gentle lover at the start, when he had to his delight and astonishment discovered her virginity, later gave way to a savagery that matched the fiery passion she had not suspected in herself. Polly's first instinct had been to fight. No man, she had vowed in Bandyleg Lane, should touch her, and the unwonted invasion of her body had aroused an innate resistance.

'I would not force you, Polly,' Charles had whispered. 'I take no woman against her will. Have no fear of me. Go home if that is your desire.' He had paused, loosening his hold on her arms and looking down at her. '*Is* it your desire?'

Sheer physical panic swept her momentarily. 'Yes, sire. Yes.' He had sighed long and deeply. 'Then, Poll—' But suddenly a flame of passion shook her body and she pulled him close to her. 'No, no!'

A light breeze wafted through the room, stirring the dying flames to life. But the logs were only ashes now, and the flicker died as soon as it was born. She slipped softly out of bed, taking care not to disturb him. Reaching in the darkness for a garment with which to cover herself, she chanced upon his discarded Chinese robe. She wrapped it round, and tiptoed to the window.

Below lay the privy stairs leading down to the river. Coral streaked the sky to the east, outlining the distant skeleton of the burned cathedral on its hillock above the City. The coral brightened and took on a nacreous sheen, as shimmering as the inner skin of a pearl's shell. On the quiet water, boats bobbed at anchor, scarcely seeming to touch the river at all, so lightly did they rest. Downstream, a slight eddy rippled about a schooner's bows, the lantern at her peak burning palely against the brightening sky.

Polly drank in the scene's cool tranquility, letting her mind play over the hectic events of the night. Now, in the quiet of the king's bedchamber, the masquerade seemed unreal. But the slow rhythm of the pavane pulsed still within her.

There was a faint sound behind her. She swung about. Was Charles awakening? No, it was not Charles. The door was moving slowly, cautiously. Polly drew herself back behind a deep fold of the window curtains. Now the door was half-open, and a woman wearing a gown of white lace quietly entered the room. Polly held her breath. It was the queen, Catherine of Braganza.

Softly the delicately-built, olive-skinned woman moved to the bedside and looked down at her sleeping husband. Her face wore an expression of sadness, and of infinite tenderness. She bent over and kissed him – a kiss as light as a butterfly's. He stirred in his sleep and murmured a word: 'Polly.' Polly saw sudden tears glitter in the queen's eyes. Turning back towards the door, Catherine brushed past a low stool; on it lay Polly's seed-pearl cap. She picked it up, smiled ruefully, and turned her face towards the curtain where Polly stood. The queen's hands, pale in the dawn glow, moved upward and outward in the unmistakable gesture of one asking pardon for having intruded. She put the cap back and glided through the door. Soundlessly it closed behind her.

Polly stared at the sleeping king. What manner of man was this, to arouse such passion in so many women, and yet to retain the love of one so long neglected, so disregarded in the busy stream of events which made up his restless days and his impassioned nights?

She studied the heavy features, so ugly and yet so magnificent, and thought of the varying bloodstreams that intertwined within those royal veins – Norman, Breton, English, Danish, Scots, French, even Italian through his grandmother, Marie de Medici. As she watched, the growing light from the window fell across the bed. One powerful arm emerged from the coverlet. Charles opened his eyes and fixed them upon her.

'Good morrow, madame,' he said with the courtesy and aplomb he might have shown had they met strolling in the Privy Garden. 'I trust you slept well? And that my clocks did not disturb you?'

His clocks? Not their chiming, she thought, nearly so much as the strangeness of his company. She did her best to curtsey in the enveloping folds of the Chinese robe.

'I slept marvellously, sire,' she lied, smiling at the concern in his eyes, the thoughtful concern of a polite host. 'And I am most grateful for your – hospitality.'

'Come back, Poll,' he said, stretching out his arms to her. ' 'Tis barely day.' She hesitated. 'No, I'll not tumble you again, I vow. But let us talk a little before the king must return to his governing.'

He lounged, propped up by pillows, his arms folded across his broad bare chest, relaxed, smiling at her. She still held back. He patted the bedside. 'Come, Poll. Must I command?'

'Oh, no, my lord!'

She crossed the room and perched at the end of the bed. This then was her moment. This was why she had been emboldened to trick her way into the palace – to warn the king: to tell him of her suspicions – the strange sordid tale of the Earl of Kinnerton, who consorted with the cut-throat, Galloping Jack; of the stench within *Fancy Anne*, of the gyves and fetters on the slave deck below. Already a murder had been committed. Mark Lampson lay dead in his own blood upon Thames-side. She opened her mouth to speak, felt her throat grow dry.

There was something almost innocent about the king, something guileless in that friendly warm smile, something invulnerable to evil. It occurred to her that Charles, far from taking any serious notice of what she had to tell, would merely laugh. Besides, what did she really know? Suppose Whipt Ned's first guess had been right, that Kinnerton was involved in nothing more than a petty affair of smuggling? Surely such breaches of the law were matters for the magistrates, and not for His Majesty.

'You wanted to say something, Poll,' Charles prompted. 'Speak on. Have no fear. No man is a king without his breeches, you know.' She still hesitated to loosen her tongue. He asked, 'Where do you live?'

'In Bandyleg Lane, so please you, sire. Hard by Halfpenny Close where –'

'Where you saved my life?'

'I knew not then you were the king.'

Charles laughed. 'What? Had you known you would have curtseyed first and meanwhile let me die?'

She flushed. 'You take me for a fool, Charles – er, sire.'

'Sire will do very well for daylight, Poll. We'll keep Charles for the night, shall we? I take you for anything but a fool. Tell me of yourself.'

So Polly began, the words crowding on, encouraged by the genuine interest in his eyes. She spoke of Granny Fitch's kitchen, of Will, her father, and of poor Whipt Ned. Charles interrupted.

'Those two were your chair-men, I'll be bound, who bore you to my Lady Castlemaine's?'

She nodded. Will had borrowed the sedan-chair from a bearer in Drury Lane whose master had fled from London when the Great Fire broke out. She had heard Charles last night, as she stood trembling after they reached his bedchamber, tell a servant to give the pair some coins and send them home.

'And the costume you wore? How did you come by that?'

Should she tell the truth? Would the king be angered at poor old Nick Farrow's lending it to her from the wardrobe of His Majesty's own theatre? But she caught a twinkle in Charles's eye.

'You need not tell me. I know already. I saw the words, Theatre Royal, sewn inside. You are no thief, Polly. So shall we say it was loaned to you – by a friend there? Now who? The theatre's empty save for old Farrow, the custodian. It seems you have power over men of all stations, lass.'

'It was no fault of Nick's,' she said quickly. 'I coaxed him.'

'And he could not resist? No, I shall not blame him. I have at least one thing in common with Nick Farrow. I can't resist female wheedling either.'

How easy Charles was to get on with. And how quick his mind. So much quicker than the dullards she had known.

The clocks chimed again. 'Time grows short,' the king said. 'Mr Chiffinch will call me soon. But I would know a little more. You have entrée to my theatre. Good. But why?'

She blurted it out.

'Because I wish to become an actress. I know I can. I am certain of it. Others – humble girls like me – have succeeded!'

'And still more have broken their foolish innocent hearts. To get up upon the stage – to face the crowds in the pit, the insolent lordlings lounging and staring and squabbling with each other – the women of the town in their vizards, far more interested in the gallants than in the play – to stand before all these cold, selfish, arrogant, self-centred, brawling, stupid people and conquer them, make them listen! Not easy, Poll, not easy! I'd rather face Cromwell's army again before the walls of Worcester town than stand alone before an audience at the Theatre Royal.'

'But you are a soldier, sire, and battle comes naturally to you.

'And you are an actress?'

She knew he was mocking her. Her eyes flashed. 'I am – or will become one.'

'Each to his own métier. 'Tis fair enough. And indeed you're a stately piece, Madame Fitch. Your body is fit enough to be a queen's – far more fit than most queens' I have known.'

'And I can read, too, sire, and write.'

'But can you guide your tongue trippingly over the poetry of our playwrights? It's there the talent lies – not in a fine pair of legs or two bright eyes alone, mistress.'

It was a challenge. 'Will it please you, sire, to listen?'

Charles nodded. 'With all my heart, Poll, so you accept me as critic. I assure you, I am exigent in that role.'

She took a deep breath. She had committed herself. But what to choose, what character to play before the king of England, in his bedchamber? No stage stretched before her, only the rumpled bedclothes. And no proscenium arched above, merely the carvings and canopy of the four-poster. And yet the bed with its hangings vaguely suggested a theatre. She decided on Viola in *Twelfth Night*, the girl in boy's clothes.

'Build me – ' She stopped: that was wrong. Charles knew what passage she had chosen, and prompted her. 'Make –'

She picked up the cue and went on calmly, her voice melodious, each word clear and meaningful.

> *'Make me a willow cabin at your gate,*
> *And call upon my soul within the house;*
> *Write loyal cantons of contemned love,*
> *And sing them loud, even in the dead of night;*
> *Holla your name to the reverberate hills,*
> *And make the babbling gossip of the air*
> *Cry out Olivia!'*

She stole a glance at her audience. He was intent, leaning slightly forward.

> *'O, you should not rest*
> *Between the elements of air and earth,*
> *But you should pity me.'*

She paused. What would he say? He surprised her.

'Would you essay another speech?'

'If I know it, sire.'

He cued her:

'*To a nunnery, go.*'

Ophelia's words came easily to her.

> *'O, what a noble mind is here o'erthrown!*
> *The courtier's, soldier's, scholar's eye, tongue, sword:*
> *The expectancy and rose of the fair state,*

59

The glass of fashion and the mould of form,
The observ'd of all observers, . . . '

She stopped abruptly. She could go no further: the poetry drew an uncanny portrait of the very man to whom she addressed it. The lines that remained of the speech – lines that described the prince's madness – had suddenly become unspeakable in that bedchamber. She dropped a curtsey.

'I have forgot the rest, my lord. I'm sorry.'

Charles rose from the bed, enveloping himself in a crimson robe. 'No matter, Poll, no matter.' He put his hands on her shoulders. 'You can bring life to words. An actress – perhaps you are right, after all. We must see what my Company of Comedians will make of you.'

His mood changed. Now he was brisk. 'I must begin my day. No more of poets and of pretty actresses. But stay, you cannot return to Bandyleg Lane in your robe of the masquerade. I'll see the dress returned to Nick, never fear. But we must find something else for you to wear.' He pondered, fondly measuring her with his eyes.

'I could obtain a gown from one of the ladies of the court, but I fear you are too tall. Your long legs would emerge beneath the hem like beanstalks. You're nigh as high as I am. Come, stand beside me.'

Side by side, they faced the mirror. She stood lean and lithe and vibrant, as unlikely a creature to have blossomed out of the slum as the astonishingly beautiful bright yellow weed – never before seen in London – that was already sprouting out of the ashes of the Great Fire. The king spoke admiringly. 'I have six feet and two inches. And our brows are almost level. Polly, my Amazon, you must be six feet tall. Will they ever find you a leading man? Still, that's Charles Hart's problem. For the moment, how shall we clothe you?'

He called out, thrusting Polly behind the curtain that had concealed her when the queen was in the room, 'Chiffinch, Will Chiffinch.' The door swung open as though Chiffinch had been listening at the keyhole.

'Good morning, sire.'

'Will, bring me – let me see – a pair of my breeches, the rough ones I use for hawking. A shirt. Hose. A hat. And a leather jerkin. Now hurry.'

'Does Your Majesty hawk? Methought there was the council.'

'No, Will, I do not hawk. No curiosity, if you please. Just bring me the garments.'

As she donned the unfamiliar male garb, Polly heard Charles, attended by Chiffinch, in the next room, laughing with his barber: 'Ah, to be a youth with ne'er a whisker on my chin.' She smiled. She knew the jest was meant for her. Dressed at last she stood before the mirror and coiled her long hair up beneath the hat. A passable youth she made, indeed, tall, strong and graceful.

So she was to become an actress – or at least she was to be given the chance. She thought, sardonically, that she had paid the very price old Nick Farrow had predicted – first the bed, and only after that, the stage. She wondered if she would ever see the king again, except in his royal box, or riding through the City while she stood among the cheering crowds. When he had said, 'Keep Charles for the night,' had he meant that one night only?

The bedchamber was filled with sunshine now, and the magic of the moon-washed hours they had shared had vanished, brushed away by the glare of a new day. Well, she had been the king's mistress for a few hours. And perhaps, it suddenly occurred to her, she might even be carrying the seed of one more royal child.

Charles strode in.

'Ah, Master Fitch, ready to depart?'

'So please you, sire.'

Will Chiffinch lingered behind the king and stared at Polly, his eyes widening in shocked surprise. She concealed a smile as Chiffinch's puzzled gaze swung from 'Master Fitch' to Charles. It was so easy to imagine what was passing through his mind: after all, the king's grandfather, James I, had been a notorious pederast.

'Will.'

'Your Majesty?'

'Please have a boat and a waterman ready for Master Fitch at the foot of the privy stairs. See him safely aboard for the City, and then return here. Meanwhile we would confer a space, before the council begins.'

Chiffinch bowed, and backed out of the room. Charles caught Polly's eye, and twinkled. He rubbed his hand over his newly-shaven jaw and winced slightly.

'I envy your pure-bred Englishman with his fine blond beard. My Italian blood produces wire!' He took Polly's chin in his hand, and tilted her face upward.

'I am sorry. I see I have scraped that delicate skin.' There were other marks, Polly thought, that he could not see – bruises hidden by the fustian and leather of her costume. 'You make a rare lad, Polly. You might indeed play Viola.' He gently unfastened the front of her jerkin and touched her breasts through the white shirt. 'But only at a distance, dear heart. Only at a distance.'

'Dear heart,' she echoed softly, smiling into his eyes. 'So tender an address.'

'My mother's to my father.' His right forefinger traced a tiny cross on his heart. 'Now, Poll, today my council consider London. It is destroyed. One must re-create it. But how? How best for the people who live in it? I should like to hear what you have to say.'

He withdrew a roll of vellum from a cabinet and spread it out on a table. 'This is a plan for the new City. It was made by one of our most learned men.' She looked with puzzlement at the spidery lines, trying to interpret them. 'Now, this is north, and this south. Here is Saint Paul's; it shall be remade in the modern style, mayhap with a dome. Here are public buildings.' His hands moved over the plan. 'Fleet Street, you see, Poll, here. And here, linking the streets, piazzas in the Italian manner, broad and sunlit. And on this site, the new Royal Exchange. It is your neighbourhood, Poll – more your world than ours. So what think you?'

She pondered over the design. It seemed the perfect dream of a great and majestic metropolis, but for her, well – not quite human enough.

'I have no skill in such matters, sire. I pray you, excuse me.'

'Nay, but it is easy to understand. Picture to yourself these lines, these angles, these avenues and squares clothed in white stone, planted out with trees and gardens. What then?'

His eyes were serious, fixed on her with concentration. She gulped. To lie, or to offend?

' 'Tis very grand. Fit for a king. For processionals and the glow of pageantry.' She paused. 'But where would the people live? And how?'

'The people.' Charles rubbed his chin. 'Aye, there's the rub of it, my sweeting.'

'Sire, we have humble wants, we Londoners. We love our twisting, secret alleys, our small houses, our inns, our taverns. But we would not have them burned to the ground again. If Your Majesty might perhaps build to prevent that?'

'But burning – it was the act of Providence. How shall I prevent it?'

'Brick does not burst into flame as the old timber did. Nor could fire o'erleap a street, if the street were wider.'

'True.'

Her self-confidence grew as she realized that he was listening – listening carefully.

'Oh, if the streets were wider, then Your Majesty's subjects would perhaps not grow up, as so many do now, stunted and crippled, like Whipt Ned and my father. If only the sun could reach their windows as it does yours!'

'What would my council know of such things?' Charles mused. ' 'Tis common sense. And yet all they can think of is domes and noble piazzas and malls. Bricks, so the town shall not burn again! Sunshine so the children shall mature straight and not crooked!'

There was a knock. Chiffinch put his head in the door. 'The boat awaits, sire.'

'In a moment, Will, in a moment.'

Chiffinch withdrew.

'I need the advice of such a one as you, Poll. Scholars and courtiers are not enough.'

'If I were king, sire – '

'Ah, but you cannot be, any more than poor François Villon who voiced the same desire in France many years ago. But you could – no, faith, I cannot make Polly Fitch a member of my council. Yet, stay – I could name you an extra lady of the court. Thus you would have access.'

'A lady to Her Majesty? The queen?' Her cheeks crimsoned at the thought.

Charles shook his head. 'That would never do. No, to Lady Charlotte Fitzroy, my daughter by Barbara Castlemaine.'

'Lady Castlemaine!'

'There would be no need for you to come face to face with her. Nor with small Charlotte either. Though she is only two – and a delight. Like you not the name? 'Tis my own, in the feminine gender. Yes, Polly, you shall be baby Charlotte's lady. And your duties will be to guide me. To advise me how best to better the lot of my poor subjects in the City of London. I will appoint quarters for you in the palace. And suitable dresses.'

He paused. 'But I command, I do not ask. A king may do so, yet it is less than courteous. Are you willing to serve me a few days, Poll, or would you off to the stage at once?'

'I would serve you, my lord, as best I can.'

'Then we shall meet again.' He called out. 'Chiffinch!'

The door opened.

'Sire?'

'See Master Fitch to his boat.'

Polly stood at the bottom of the privy stairs. Water lapped greenly over the stone. The boat drew up. Chiffinch waited to hand his master's guest aboard. She caught the look in his eye, as incredulous as before.

'I give you good day, Master Chiffinch,' she said. And then, as she stepped into the rocking craft and turned to wave goodbye, she purposely let her jerkin swing open. Chiffinch stared where he was meant to stare, and his face cleared. He bowed low to the sweetest smile that morning in London. After all, she owed it to Charles.

Gracefully, the small boat glided downstream. Polly did not

observe the slim dark man who watched from the battlements above. The Earl of Kinnerton too had seen the swelling womanhood beneath the jerkin. Had seen, and would remember.

CHAPTER VI

FESTIVAL OF KNAVES

To Polly Fitch, what she had glimpsed of Whitehall Palace on her way to the small chambers she had been given, was a bewildering labyrinth. Long corridors, all looking much the same to her, with their portraits and their gilded furniture and their gigantic candelabra, intersected unexpectedly; panels swung open to reveal hidden doors; twisting staircases secretly linked floor with floor, narrow passageway with narrow passageway. And everywhere there was a constant press of people.

For the first two days she had waited in her quarters, scarcely daring to stir out for a moment, lest she miss a command to attend the king. But no one came for her, no one even spoke to her, except the servants who brought her meals. That was all just as well: she would as soon not be seen in her poor faded dress, the only one she owned. She was quite the lady in it, in Bandyleg Lane; but it was pathetically laughable among the splendidly-fashioned gowns worn every day by the women in Whitehall.

At last, on the third morning, a young man knocked at her door.

'Mistress Fitch?'

She curtseyed. He was tall, though not so tall as Charles, and his features were fine-drawn. His was a manly, aristocratic face, and, when she rose and looked into the grey eyes, she saw that it was kindly too.

'I am Bartelmy Ravenscroft. I have the honour to be one of His Majesty's Gentlemen of the Bedchamber. Would it be convenient for you to come with me?'

'Indeed, sir.'

He ushered her through the crowds in the Stone Gallery, past a pair of warders who guarded a velvet-draped entrance and into a silent corridor. They walked through a string of rooms hung with sombre paintings, one opening into the next, and finally stopped beside a broad mullioned window that gave a panoramic view of the sparkling Thames.

'You are to wait here, if you please, mistress,' said Bart. Within a few seconds he was back.

'Her Majesty will see you now.'

She felt a coldness at the pit of her stomach. The queen! Had Her Majesty learned that it was she who spent that night with Charles? She stumbled as she crossed the room and entered another larger one.

'Mistress Fitch, Your Majesty.'

Polly sank into a deep curtsey, her eyes on the carpet. She could not bring herself to lift them. For a few seconds there was absolute silence; to the embarrassed girl they seemed like hours. She could see nothing but the elaborate twisting patterns of the carpet, but she felt the queen's eyes upon her.

'You may rise, child.'

She straightened and looked at last at Catherine of Braganza, who sat in a low chair beside a table on which lay several dresses.

'Thank you, Master Ravenscroft,' the queen said. 'You may leave us now.'

'Does Your Majesty wish me to wait to guide Mistress Fitch back to her quarters?'

'One of my ladies can do that.'

Bart Ravenscroft bowed.

'Very good, Your Majesty.'

He withdrew. The latch clicked behind him. Polly was alone with the queen of England.

'Your name is Polly, is it not?'

Catherine's speech still retained a delicate shadow of soft Portuguese. The girl nodded.

'Then may I call you Polly?'

The question was so gently voiced that Polly felt a bitter twinge of guilt at how grossly she had betrayed this strangely unassuming royal lady.

'If it please Your Majesty.'

Catherine smiled. 'Just "madame" will do. I understand I

have reason to be grateful to you.'

'To me?' Polly was staggered. Surely Catherine had every reason to feel the opposite.

'You saved the king's life during the fire. He told me of it. And so did his brother, the Duke of York. I am most grateful. And now you are to serve the king again – him and his people – by helping him plan how best to rebuild our beloved London. That is why I sent for you.'

'To –'

'My husband considered that you might be in need of –' the sensitive smile touched her face again 'of some garments suitable to this place. I'm afraid it was necessary to keep you waiting in your chambers until they could be made ready. You are so very tall, you see, and there was nothing of mine or my ladies that would have fitted. I hope you are pleased, Polly.'

The next quarter of an hour was bewildering. With the queen's aid, she undressed and tried on her new gowns – one of an intense blue that mirrored the colour of her eyes; one of a vibrant emerald green; one of an amber hue; one of deep red. She fingered the lustrous silks, the laces with sensuous delight. These were fabrics so unlike anything she had ever touched before!

It was unbelievable – the queen helping her to adjust the intricate corslets, kneeling to straighten her skirt, to smooth a fold away, as if she were the royal personage and the other only a maid.

Finally the queen rose and stood back.

Polly was radiant in the rustling blue silk.

'There.' An eager smile swept Catherine's face, and she spoke almost anxiously, like a little girl. 'Do you like them?'

Polly stammered. 'They are beautiful. You are so kind, madame. What can I say?'

'Nay, you must thank the king, not I. They fit well, do they not?'

'Oh, wondrously.'

'For that too you must thank His Majesty. He borrowed a gown from the Theatre Royal which someone told him you had once worn. Are you then an actress, child?'

'Not yet, madame. One day I hope to be.' Polly remembered the seed-pearl cap. The thought crept into her mind that the queen was now giving a better performance than ever she had seen on any stage. Surely she was not so innocent as not even to suspect. Somehow, Polly was certain little slipped past Catherine of Braganza.

'You will wear this one then? Good. And I shall have the others sent to your chambers.' Catherine's voice took on a grave note. 'You are to be here some little while, I believe. Would a few words of advice come amiss?'

'Oh, no, madame. Truly not. I should treasure them.'

'If by treasure you mean, put away and hoard, I beg you don't. Please act upon them. You will meet many men and women in Whitehall, Polly. Give each, as the English Shakespeare wrote, your ear, but few your tongue. And study carefully that which you may hear. There are good men and women in the palace, but there are liars and tricksters and fools as well. The king will not lie to you, nor will I. Nor I think will that sometimes ill-tempered, but always so sad little man, Lord Clarendon. He is the most loyal friend a king ever had. If only Charles knew it!

'But there are others, Polly, of whom you cannot feel so sure. Seeing that you hold a place of trust, even if briefly, they will try to use you. Beware of them, and commit yourself to nothing.'

'Whitehall –' she hesitated, searching for the word, 'it resembles what the Flemish people call a *Kermesse*, a festival. But it is no ordinary festival. Here the game is for money and power and influence. It is a festival of knaves. Will you remember that?'

Polly nodded.

'Then go with God,' said the queen. 'You are not, of course, of the true religion?' She meant Roman Catholic.

Polly shook her head, reddening in embarrassment.

'No, of course not. Still, accept a Catholic queen's blessing. Be true to England, and to the king.' She picked up a tiny silver handbell and tinkled it. The door opened and a comely young woman entered and bobbed.

'This is the Lady Margaret Carfax. Her ladyship will escort you to the council chamber.'

Polly curtseyed, feeling the unaccustomed richness of the heavy silken skirt move with her body.

'Thank you, Your Majesty.'

She backed to the door, her eyes fixed on the queen – devout, loving and appealingly humble. How lonely she looked, silhouetted against the riverside window.

On the floor lay the bedraggled, worn-out dress that Polly had brought from Bandyleg Lane.

Charles's council sat in the Palace of Westminster, next door to Whitehall, in the ancient Star Chamber whose ceiling, with its now faded painted stars, had given the room its name, once the synonym for cruel and barbarous trials. Lady Margaret Carfax had delivered Polly to Bart Ravenscroft in a small dark anteroom. After disappearing into the council, he reappeared to nod in a reassuring way.

A moment later, she stood facing the king. He sat at the head of a sombre group of men around a long oaken table, strewn with documents and drawings. She spotted among them the new London plan he had shown her that dawn in his bed-chamber.

Charles turned to the others.

'Gentlemen, may I present Mistress Fitch who was of some good service to me in the City during the fire? Mistress Fitch, my brother, the Duke of York.'

James, with his fine features and high-strung pale good looks, so unlike his brother's swarthy masculinity, smiled faintly. 'We have met before, Mistress Fitch, I think.' She recognized the agitated, smoke-streaked young man of Half-penny Close.

Then she tried, between curtseys, to make mental notes on the rest, so that she would remember them as the king pro-nounced their names. Lord Clarendon – short, unhealthily plump, a straggling beard, aging, an air of mocking skepticism in his curt nod; Dr Christopher Wren, the architect – a keen glance, youngish, whimsical; John Evelyn – thin-lipped, bony-

nosed, intellectual, faintly disapproving of everyone else; the
Earl of Kinnerton, lounging, languid, his sharp gaze seeming
to pierce her as if to ferret out her secrets.

And one other: 'My son, the Duke of Monmouth.' She had
seen young Jemmie before, dancing with a grace that almost
matched his father's, at Lady Castlemaine's masquerade.
Jemmie looked her up and down with a bold, appraising openly
sexual stare that also almost matched his father's.

She wondered who were to be her friends, who her enemies.
She remembered what the queen had said about Clarendon
and, despite his somewhat grumpy expression, marked him
down as friend. Dr Wren too looked inviting, though she
feared that he would be too intelligent for her to follow his
thoughts. Evelyn worried her far more seriously: did his
general scorn of the others include her too, even before he knew
her? The Duke of York seemed welcoming enough, but
remote, a man who would do no overt harm, but whose private
worries would always take first place, whose interest in others
must inevitably be slight.

As for the Duke of Monmouth, she summed him up quickly:
ambitious, vain and for the moment wondering, she guessed,
if his father had lain with her, and if where his father had
explored he might not as well find hidden treasure.

Monmouth spoke: 'I trust you are comfortable in this old
place.'

'Indeed I am, sir.'

He glanced at her, sidelong: 'You must show me your
rooms, mistress. Mayhap they may need some added refine-
ment that I could provide.'

Charles's dark thoughtful eyes twinkled. He said softly,
'Careful, Jemmie.'

The interchange was not lost on Kinnerton. His snakelike
hooded eyes flickered from the king to the bastard, then fell to
the table. He began to scribble on a scrap of paper.

Charles motioned Polly to a vacant chair, and Bart stood
attentively behind her.

'Both Wren and Evelyn,' said Charles, addressing the group,
'have prepared plans for a new London. You gentlemen have

studied them. But the question that arises – with all due respect to the immense skill and learning of both – is this. Have they not perhaps concentrated overmuch on, shall I say, the pomposities, the pageantries of our royal capital? I will not say to the detriment of everyday living, but perhaps the emphasis might well be adjusted.'

Evelyn said, 'As Your Majesty pleases. London rebuilt should be rebuilt to the glory of God. For it was assuredly God who destroyed our modern Sodom and levelled it like unto the Cities of the Plain.'

'God,' growled Clarendon querulously, 'speaking either French or Hollandish.'

'Nay,' said Charles, bringing his hand smartly down on the table, 'Sodom we may have been, John Evelyn, but if so, Sodom we always were and shall continue far beyond the span of our own poor lives. What is in the nature of the beast, that will surely remain.

'As for our foes across the channel, my lord earl, you do them too much honour, and credit them with too wise and skilful a malice.'

Clarendon shrugged.

Charles continued, 'Unless, Dr Evelyn, all accidents are the acts of a just God – and I cannot equate justice with vengeful-ness to be sure, though I am of course no theologian – it might be more sensible simply to say that what happened began by mischance in my own baker's ovens in Pudding Lane. Thence, by continued mischance, and neither by divine nor foreign intervention, the flames spread from house to house.'

'Perhaps,' drawled Kinnerton, 'Mistress Fitch has a view. How say you, mistress – God, the Dutch or bad luck?'

Charles nodded, signalling her to say what she chose. At first, faltering and hesitant, then with growing self-assurance, Polly began to speak.

'Bad luck, sire. If your Majesty knew the poor hovels of the City as I and my friends do, you would know that sooner or later what happened would have had to happen.

'Nay, gentlemen, pile me up together dried old beams, wooden walls and thatch for hundreds of years. Subject them

to a scorching wind and burning sun without a spatter of rain
for months on end. Then let some poor wretch – baker or
tallow-chandler or merely a good wife – drop but a single
spark. And fire must surely follow.

'Then with nowhere nigh enough pumps and a Lord Mayor
so terrified he knows not where to turn, what is bad to begin
with speedily becomes worse and –'

She stopped, abashed. She had spoken ill of Charles's Lord
Mayor. Had she gone too far?

'Fear not, mistress,' said Charles. 'My Lord Mayor indeed
quaked and quivered and failed to lead his people. But I'll
be bound, he was no worse than thousands of others might
have been. There are few sights that bring on so great a panic
as the sight of leaping flames.

'Well then, the City was ripe for fire. What now? How to
prevent another such accident – or divine visitation, if you
prefer, Dr Evelyn?'

Evelyn's lips tightened, 'You jest at God, Your Majesty?'

Charles shook his head. 'Nay, I do not. For 'tis with His
will alone that I rule this nation. I do but jest a little at you,
good sir. But with all due respect for your many gifts, which I
cherish as much as those of any man in all England.'

How adroit he was, Polly thought, as she watched Evelyn's
prickly temper abate and soften, soothed by his monarch's
tact.

'Sire,' said Dr Christopher Wren, 'as you know, I am
proceeding apace with my plans. St Paul's alone will take us a
decade's work or more. And there must be other churches –
many more – close at hand to the worshippers. Livery halls
and, too, sire, public buildings. But I cannot possibly create
them, not even in my mind, until I know what are the necessities, the essentials, within which to set these jewels.'

'In your opinion, mistress, what are these necessities?'

Necessities! Polly Fitch had dreamt of nothing but necessities throughout her seventeen years on earth. Good food,
dry warm rooms, clean water, sunshine, space in which to live
and grow.

Again she began to speak, calmly, convincingly, telling the

courtiers and the learned men of an existence they had never known, and could not have imagined even in the most penurious days of the king's exile. She conjured up a picture of her own childhood: hunger, cold, filth, illness; the savagery of the hard-pressed poor, one preying upon the next; plague spreading from body to body huddled together on dank straw beds; babies born amid rats and lice. Shameful lives and sordid deaths.

Finally she stopped, breathless. Her narrative, enunciated in the rough passionate language of Bandyleg Lane, had spared her hearers nothing. And it had lifted Polly herself far away from the Star Chamber and all the strange wonderland of the royal court. Now, as she took in the faces before her, she returned to reality. Her hearers had been swept along by her words, of that there was no doubt.

Old Clarendon was visibly moved: a tear glinted in one eye. Wren, rubbing his chin, stared thoughtfully at the dully-gleaming stars on the ceiling. Evelyn sat diligently writing notes. Kinnerton surveyed her with keen speculation, seemingly pondering a question to which he could find no answer.

As for the king, his heavy features were impassive; his large hands rested upon the table motionless. He looked about, his eyebrows raised interrogatively.

Evelyn said, 'I've pleaded before this, sire, about the fouling of the air. Perhaps now, we might group the tanners and meat-smokers and fish-curers separately, away from dwelling places?'

Dr Wren murmured, 'Wider streets. I must redraft my plans . . .'

Suddenly they were all talking at once, eddies of words overlapping, creating cross-currents of thoughts, wavelets of emotion. Polly felt as if she had dropped a stone into a quiet pool.

'You merit our thanks, mistress,' said Charles at last. 'What you have told us is not new – but, likewise, it had not been said so fervently before. You may be assured your time is not wasted. Nor will your passion be without issue.'

Polly rose and made a reverence.

'You honour me, Your Majesty.'

'Master Ravenscroft,' the king said, 'will you be kind enough to escort Mistress Fitch again to Whitehall?'

Bart bowed and, together, he and Polly backed out of the Star Chamber.

That night she saw for the first time the true splendour of Whitehall, when Bart arrived to escort her to a banquet the king was giving for the new Russian ambassador. The feast, on gold plate, and with so many courses that Polly soon lost count of them, was served at long tables in the Banqueting House beneath the glorious ceiling that Rubens had painted to celebrate the virtues of Charles's most unvirtuous grandfather.

As she entered, Polly stood stock-still, trying to encompass the breathtaking beauty of it all – the walls and columns gleaming white-and-gilt, the lofty windows richly curtained. Musicians played in the gallery above. She had not dreamed that the whole world held so many jewels as now glistened in the candle-light.

The Russian sat with the king and queen at a table raised above the others. What was that stuff that edged the ambassador's robe, she wondered. Could it be the fur called sable?

Bart took her to a chair beside the Earl of Kinnerton. He raised his ornate Venetian goblet to her: 'A toast to the new beauty in Whitehall!'

Polly replied, 'Nay, my lord earl, I'm no Whitehall beauty, but simply one whose views are sought by His Majesty.'

'And when he has ascertained all your views, mistress, you return to – where is it, now – Bandyleg Lane?'

She nodded, amused at his pretended ignorance of a region with which she knew him to be well acquainted.

'What a pity. For so statuesque a goddess to come to us, only to leave us. We have few of so splendid a *taille* here. Indeed, I have seen only one such in all my time at court.'

'Indeed, sir?'

He looked down into the darkness of the wine in his goblet, and then spoke softly. ' 'Twas at Lady Castlemaine's masque. An unknown fair who arrived unbidden, dressed all in black like Queen Mary of the Scots. Later, it is said, she bedded with

75

the king.'

There were, Polly reflected, prying eyes, as the queen had warned, in Whitehall. Had Kinnerton followed them to the Privy Garden and seen Charles unmask her?

' 'Tis passing strange, is it not,' he went on, 'that there should be just such another, tall and stately as yourself, madame, and within only a few days?'

'Strange,' she replied, 'but not, my lord, impossible.'

He drew closer to her and spoke in an undertone. 'Come, Polly, you can tell me. Are we not friends?'

'Are we? How could we be on so short an acquaintance?'

'We are drawn together by a common bond. Do we not both serve the king, each in his own way? Come, please reveal yourself. It was you, was it not, at my Lady Castlemaine's?'

'Pray forgive me, my lord, if I tell you that you are mistaken.'

He sipped his wine. 'Ah, well, perchance it may be so. By the bye, have you a brother?'

'I? No indeed, my lord. Why do you ask?'

He shrugged. 'I saw a tall slim youth, in breeches and jerkin, depart by boat from the privy stairs. Your image, Polly, I swear.'

She waited.

'The morning after my Lady Castlemaine's masquerade.' He paused, also waiting. 'And the boat sped east.'

She wondered if she might not turn this fencing match against Kinnerton. What if she were to speak just two words: *Fancy Anne*?

As she hesitated – it might be a foolish risk – the king and queen rose, and all the company rose with them. Bart came to her side. 'Mistress Fitch, may I accompany you?'

She took his arm, saying good night over her shoulder to Kinnerton. He bowed and gave her a mocking smile. 'We shall meet again, Polly, shall we not?'

'Only if,' she replied as she moved away, 'it is His Majesty's pleasure, my lord earl.'

She had no idea where she had found the courage to say such a thing to such a man.

CHAPTER VII

THE SHADOW OF THE BASTARD

Sunset struck through the casement windows of the Duke of Monmouth's chambers beyond King Street, near the Cock Pit Theatre, casting the young man's long shadow across the floor. Jemmie stared gloomily at the insubstantial shifting image of himself. He raised his arm. The shadow's arm moved as if in a mocking salute. He dropped it. Kinnerton, who sat sipping a flagon of wine in a deep window embrasure, watched amused. 'So, Jemmie, what mean these motions?'

The king's son swung towards him, his face pale, his eyes snapping with anger.

'I study my shadow, Kinnerton, because that is all I am. Shadow of a man. Shadow of a monarch. My father raises his arm – so – and the world stops to listen and to obey. I raise mine, and what response does the bastard receive? Only the empty salute of a shadow!'

Kinnerton surveyed his young friend with a touch of scorn.

'Your day will come, Jemmie.'

'But when? When? Ah, yes, he calls me Duke of Monmouth. But of what am I truly duke? An empty title! King Charles speaks, and a hundred ships of war leap from their moorings. He whispers, and beautiful women vie to strip themselves naked. Thus it is to be a king.'

'You have no lack of feminine adulation.'

'But why? Only that these sluts may, through me, come closer to my sovereign lord. And once they achieve this, I am forgotten and the king's is their only bed.'

He paused. 'Who is this Mistress Fitch?'

'Your father's most recent fancy, I believe.'

Monmouth flushed with royal anger.

'You are impertinent, my lord earl.'

Kinnerton was genuinely astonished. 'I, Jemmie?'

'When you refer to His Majesty, refer to him properly. You

presume too much on our friendship.'

'My humblest apologies, Your Royal Highness.'

'Nay, and no sarcasm either. Time enough for royal-highnessing when the moment arrives. But what mean you, that Polly Fitch is a fancy of the king's?'

Kinnerton shrugged. 'You attended the council, Jemmie. You saw for yourself with what attention His Majesty listened to her every word.'

'But that does not make her his bedfellow. What proof have you?'

'None, for an absolute certainty. But on the night of Lady Castlemaine's rout, there was a tall woman in black.'

Jemmie was startled. 'She?'

'How many women as tall as Polly Fitch have we in White-hall?'

'Why, no other, I suppose. But –'.

'Later His Majesty unmasked the lady in the Privy Garden by the sundial.'

'And it was she?'

'I was far off. By the wall on the King Street side. The moon was half hidden. Yet I could swear –' He stopped in mid-sentence, and then went on ominously. 'Jemmie, there is mischief here. She is the old beldame's granddaughter.'

'What old beldame?'

Kinnerton was impatient. 'Oh, come lad, you know perfectly well. The hag in Bandyleg Lane – the one they call Granny Fitch.'

Jemmie paced nervously, biting his lip.

'Then mayhap she is not merely the king's wench, but his spy as well. Women have played such parts ere this.'

Kinnerton gave him a worried look. 'But would he flaunt her thus? And even if she were in his employ, 'tis no concern of yours.'

'Not of mine? By God's body, my lord, a spy that links the City with Whitehall is indeed my concern. Whose more so?'

The earl rose and filled a flagon for Monmouth. 'Here, Jemmie lad. Cool yourself with good Rhenish wine. No matter what this lass may prove to be, you must show no worry.

Indeed you must have naught to do with the matter. Your friends shall see to such riddles for you. Keep your hands unsullied. Curb even your curiosity.

'Thus when our day comes, no blame will cling to you. Remember, you act for the good of your people. And, like Caesar's wife, you must be free of all suspicion. Leave Mistress Fitch to me. I'll wrest her secrets from her.'

'And if she truly be the king's spy? And she tells my father of your – wresting?'

Kinnerton's lips set in a hard ugly line. 'Before she can do that, I'll seal her mouth. The dead don't bite, Jemmie. There's room for her where Mark Lampson went.'

The sun by now had dropped behind the chimneys and turrets of Whitehall. The bastard and the earl were cloaked in purpling twilight.

In a far corner of the palace a small withdrawing room was still lit by the last slanting rays, for its windows faced west. The towers of Westminster Abbey showed black against the fading glow. Bart Ravenscroft sat at a spinet, gazing with admiration at Polly Fitch, who stood watching the sunset. She was magnificent in her new green gown. Bart smiled to himself, struck a thin plangent note and sang.

> *My love, my love, you do me wrong*
> *To cast me off discourteously –*
> *For I have loved thee so long,*
> *Delighting in thy company . . .*

Polly turned to look at his young handsome face, so sensitive, so humorous, so manly. How far she was, thought she, from Bandyleg Lane, with this gallant playing her so thinly disguised a serenade of love.

> *For Greensleeves is all my joy*
> *And Greensleeves is my delight –*
> *Greensleeves is my heart of gold,*
> *And who but my Lady Greensleeves!*

79

His fingers fell still upon the keys, then he repeated the last line in a soft whisper.

And who but my Lady Greensleeves!

How caressing a voice, Polly reflected, and how delightfully courteous this mode of wooing. She remembered poor Whipt Ned, flushed with drink and passion, stumbling to grasp her amid the smoke and noise of Granny Fitch's kitchen. And she thought too of Charles's self-confident love-making, his royal magnetic impetuous embrace while the spaniels whined in the corner and the fire flickered on the hearth.

Why had she been unable, that night, to tell the king of her suspicions? And why had she continued silent? Was it that, each time she had met him since, he had seemed so remote, so important, so powerful, so much a king, so little a friend? It was as if he buried the private side of his nature deliberately, the better to rule his turbulent people.

Yet she knew that the king must be informed. But how to approach him? She felt an overmastering need to confide in someone. And then instinct provided the answer: there at the spinet sat the one man whose advice she could trust.

'Bart,' she said gravely, 'I have a serious matter within my knowledge. But I am ignorant of the ways of this court. I have no means of knowing what it is right to do.'

Bart crossed the room and drew her to a window seat.

'Share it with me, dearest Polly.'

'The queen warned me,' she began stumblingly, 'that Whitehall is a festival of knaves. Do you agree?'

'I do.'

'Who, think you, is the greatest knave of all?'

Bart laughed. 'There are so many, sweet Poll. You may have your choice.'

She hesitated. He took her hand. 'Where does your own choice alight?'

She liked the feeling of his gentle grasp, his strong fingers now entwining her own. Reluctantly, she eased her hand from his.

'What say you, Bart, to my lord of Kinnerton?'

'You aim high! They say he has the sharpest wit of any man in the kingdom. Look you how he can insult His Majesty with scurrilous verse – even bait my Lady Castlemaine which none other in Whitehall dares to do, fearing the king's displeasure.

'And yet the king remains his friend, and my Lady Castlemaine, who forgives little else, forgives him his venomous verses. The king has sent him upon delicate missions to Paris and to the Hague, missions where only tact and wiliness will triumph.

'You must tread carefully, Polly. Such men, clothed with the power of state and of council, can be as virulent as vipers. But why do you choose his lordship as your prince of knaves?'

'Listen, Bart, and I'll tell you.' Then she paused, realizing that she had no right to imperil his own position. 'But you too are a courtier, and would retain the king's favour. Would you prefer not to be burdened with my knowledge?'

Bart was still boy enough for his blood to boil at the implied affront.

'Nay, Poll, if you think no more of me than that – that 'I would rather not know if a king's man is a villain than hamper my own upward path to glory in the court – then let us say farewell to each other now. In that event, I could not, surely, be worthy of –' he paused, and the heat suddenly drained from his voice 'of my Lady Greensleeves.'

This time it was Polly's hand that sought out Bart's. He was angry, and rightly so. She leaned forward and kissed him lightly on the lips.

'No hurt was meant thee, Bart. In my world, even as in Whitehall, men fight foully for advancement. I mistook you, but only for a moment. Am I forgiven?'

'If you pay forfeit, madame.'

She touched his mouth. 'But I have paid it already.'

'If I am to be the judge, I double the sentence.' He ran his fingers lightly over her face. 'Come, sweet culprit.'

She allowed a second kiss. Hers was warmer and more responsive than she had intended. She drew back.

'Bart, I would speak to you of the king's honour.'

'Which I value,' Bart replied swiftly, 'even more than I do

my own. Speak, Polly.'

She told her story in the blunt language of the streets, beginning with Whipt Ned's first sight of Kinnerton and Mark Lampson together – so unlikely a pair – in Granny Fitch's kitchen. Then she spoke of Ned's having recognized the earl in the Stone Gallery. And she went on relentlessly to the sinister murder of Mark Lampson at the waterside and, almost breathless by then, to the meeting with Captain Pargiter aboard *Fancy Anne*.

When she was done, Bart, who had listened with sharp attention, spoke slowly.

'There are cross-currents here, Poll, such as one sometimes encounters at sea. They move beneath the surface like muscles beneath the skin.'

He pondered. 'What was the merchandise from the Low Countries that this Pargiter brought aboard *Fancy Anne*? What can it be? You say you went down to the slave deck. You saw nothing?'

'It was empty.'

'No bales? No barrels?'

'Nothing, Bart. Only the chains and manacles for the poor black wretches.'

'It might be gold. In the captain's cabin. To reward someone for some deed done, or still to be done. Yet I doubt that. Nor, from what you have told me, does it appear to do with smuggling. Whipt Ned was wrong, I think.' He paused. 'He must be a rare man of his hands, this Ned of yours!'

A rueful smile touched Polly's lips. 'He is no more than one of our people, like others among the lanes where I was born. A poor man, ignorant and a bit wild.'

'But brave,' Bart commented. 'And loyal. He loves you, Polly, does he not?'

'Loves me? Yes. But he demands little – only my friendship which he will always have.'

Bart reverted to the main point. 'What is Pargiter's merchandise? What has he brought that my lord of Kinnerton values so much that he will do murder to safeguard the secret? Is there treachery here – treason in some fashion?'

Treason. The word reverberated in his memory. Lord Clarendon had used it when he spoke of Kinnerton's caustic little verse about Lady Castlemaine and her new-found Catholic faith: 'A whiff of treason.'

'What manner of man is Galloping Jack?' Bart asked Polly.

'Broad and muscular. With dark hair. And a scar.'

'Somewhere I have seen such a one. Let me think.'

He walked to the spinet and struck a chord or two absent-mindedly, then turned.

'I *have* seen such a man. This very one, mayhap. But not in England. A year past when the king sent Kinnerton to the Hague, I was dispatched after him, as a courier, a King's Messenger, with papers from the council for my lord. There was a dark man, with a scar, who galloped into the stables behind Kinnerton's quarters while I was seeing to my own mare. But I cannot be sure until I set eyes on the man himself. It was said that he had served Cromwell, as an agent, while His Majesty languished in exile in the Low Countries.'

'An agent of Cromwell, Bart? Then that could mean –'

Bart shook his head impatiently. 'Nothing, perhaps. Many of Cromwell's minions, once their cause was lost, have come over to the king. Men who will work for pay for or against any principle.

'There is Sir George Downing, for one. He spied for the Lord Protector against the king, and before that, against the king's father. Yet, when he sensed that the Commonwealth's days were numbered, he thought little of betraying his former colleagues to win himself a favoured place. He hunted down three of the old king's murderers – one, his own commander – and saw them hanged in London. Thus he proved his bona-fides. There were many like Downing in that topsy-turvy time.'

'Then for Galloping Jack to be in the Hague might signify nothing.'

'I didn't say that. We are at war with the Dutch. Captain Pargiter speaks of Dutch merchandise. *Fancy Anne* lay off in Holland during the fire and here are Galloping Jack and Kinnerton together aboard the ship – Kinnerton, remember, who served His Majesty in the Hague.'

'What did they want Mark Lampson to do that frightened him so?'

'It was the topping cove he feared.' His brow wrinkled. 'Polly, here is a thought to consider: Kinnerton has been seen much of late with the Duke of Monmouth. It all adds up to something, but the sum of so many matters escapes me.'

'Then, Bart, shall I tell the king? And will you help me?'

Bart looked doubtful. 'Indeed His Majesty should know. And yet what have we truly to tell him? Suspicions only, and those vague. A wild tale of a courtier seen aboard a slave ship. This is not a criminal act. His Majesty himself has chartered the company for the trade in blacks.'

'But what of Mark Lampson's murder?'

'That is *indeed* a crime. Yet Lampson could not have been the first ruffian to feel the prick of a courtier's sword between his ribs. Besides, let the king but command Kinnerton's apprehension for Lampson's murder, and the rest of the plot – if plot there be – dissolves into thin air, only to be reconstituted by some other traitor in the future. No, Polly, we must have more facts before the Earl of Kinnerton is seized. But how to get them?'

Polly said, 'It is not for you, Bart, to unravel the answer. Where I come from, you would stand out like a peacock in a hen-yard.'

Bart Ravenscroft walked to a high oaken press, opened it and reached inside. His hand came out with a small dagger. 'You have no weapon, Polly?'

'And why should I?'

'Because you have entered dangerous ground. I shall help you as best I can, but if we are to present the true case against Kinnerton to King Charles, the facts must be, as you say, discovered in your own world. And you may need protection.'

She took the tiny weapon and examined it.

'It seems so small.'

' 'Twill reach a man's heart, if need be.'

Polly turned her back, lifted her skirt and concealed the dagger in the top of her stocking.

Back in her own quarters Polly looked in despair through her small but elegant court wardrobe. Where in all Whitehall could she find such a tattered costume as she had worn when she arrived from Bandyleg Lane? Not even the poorest of the kitchen maids went about in such beggarly attire. Then, behind the hanging gowns she saw her answer: the king's breeches and jerkin. She had brought them in a bundle, meaning to return them to Will Chiffinch, but the chance had not arisen. Better a man's garments than the splendour of Bart's beloved Greensleeves. She changed swiftly, feeling a forgotten freedom in the easy-fitting clothes. Then she thrust Bart's tiny dagger into her waistband beneath the jerkin.

It was dark. She slipped through a side exit and blended quickly into the moving throngs that filled torchlit King Street.

In Granny Fitch's cellar, the huge kitchen, though crowded with the usual assemblage of clapperdogeons and ruffians, was strangely quiet. Whipt Ned spoke to Will Fitch in a worried undertone.

'She's a madcap wench, Ned,' said Will, laying his hand consolingly on the other's shoulder. 'She'll be back. Mayhap she's joined a band of strolling players. She has always yearned after play-acting. Does she not run off to the king's theatre whenever she has a farthing to call her own?'

'Aye,' said Ned, 'and I have been there and asked old Nick, the doorman, when last he saw her. He swore it has not been for many and many a day. But then, he may have lied.'

'I said she'd be back, Ned, and depend on it, she will, when her latest prank is o'er and done with.'

'I heard talk of a tall youth who came here the day after Polly left us. Early in the morning, it was said, he entered this place, but has not been seen again.'

Will shook his head. 'I saw no youth. Gran, did you see a tall fellow here?'

Granny Fitch busied herself with tapping a barrel of ale. She did not reply, only dropped her eyes.

'The day after we took her to my Lady Castlemaine's. Mayhap she's still in Whitehall. Or in the Tower of London. A prisoner. My pate is addled. I'm fair distracted.

'I fear her life is in danger. She and I together came on Mark Lampson ere the last breath had scarce left his body. What if his murderers saw us? And sent the tall youth here to spy out her name and her whereabouts?'

Jem Hoskin sauntered over, a brimming tankard of ale in his hand. He feigned casualness, but his genuine concern showed through his bantering words. 'Still yearning after the lost mort, Ned?'

Ned spilled out his suspicions and worries. Jem listened, his head cocked to one side, his dark eyes sharply speculative. His reaction was direct and to the point: 'Look you, Ned, it's up to us then, is it not? *We* must find this tall youth. If indeed he did come here, he may well live hard by. Why do we wait? We'll scour every alley and all the fire ruins. We'll ferret him out and drag him back here. If he knows aught, he'll speak. It'll cost him dear to try and hold his tongue.'

'And if he be not hard by at all, Jem, but elsewhere, far away?'

'Then,' Jem replied logically, 'we shall know that much, and that we must cast our nets wider.' He turned to the others and raised his voice.

'Listen, all. Ned's of opinion our Polly's been snatched away, or perhaps worse – perhaps even snuffed out. Who here has set eyes on a tall youth' he paused. 'What's he like, Ned, broad, strong, bearded?'

'Nay, none of those,' he growled. 'Slim, with a smooth, fresh cheek, like an actor – or a pimp, mayhap.'

'Now, lads,' Jem Hoskin shouted, 'scatter, do ye hear? All of you! And mind Ned's words – tall, slim. A fresh cheek. Scatter abroad, I say, and bring the rascal in.'

Something that was almost a cheer broke out. Thieves and tricksters though they were, they had all feared for Polly's safety. Two or three only had entertained another thought – that Polly, like many another lovely poor girl, had made her way from a hovel to the bedchamber of some merchant or rich noble.

86

Granny Fitch, who had been mopping up a puddle of ale from the stained stone floor, now turned towards the men. Her old crone's face, ugly and wrinkled though it was, took on an astonishing resemblance to Polly's, as a mocking smile touched her mouth and lit the rheumy eyes.

'Fools,' she said sharply. 'You'll find no slim young man. And I'll tell you why. Because no such youth exists. You play at huntsmen like so many small boys – but believe me, the fox you seek has gone to cover. Or perhaps he is not a fox! Not a fox at all!'

'We shall lay our traps, good wife,' said poor Whipt Ned angrily. 'If there be a fox, we'll drive him to earth.'

'You know not whereof you speak,' Granny Fitch was scornful. 'I tell you 'tis no fox, but an egg from which comes a butterfly.'

Will strode across to his mother.

'What are you hinting at, mam?' he demanded. 'You said you knew of no youth. Yet now you speak of him in some other guise.' He stared at her closely. 'Do you wot of something that I, Polly's father, should be party to?'

'I know naught,' Granny Fitch mumbled. 'Go to. Play at your foolish chase, son Will, you and your friends. But I tell you, you'll find no young man.'

The door opened. Jem Hoskin leaped up the stairs, shouting, 'No young man, eh? Then what's this? A ghost?' He reached out to grasp the lean figure in breeches and jerkin, but instead found himself spinning back.

'Seize him,' Will bellowed. A dozen pairs of hands reached out, but pulled back quickly as the blade of a small dagger flashed.

'Are you mad, Jem Hoskin?' cried Polly, pushing the snarling circle of men away. 'And you, Whipt Ned? Don't you know me?'

'By all the thundering gods, by Beelzebub and by Satan,' Will Fitch's voice cracked, 'It's Poll. It's my own born daughter.'

'And who else?' Polly replied, sheathing her dagger and descending the steps into the room.

Whipt Ned grasped her hand, and kissed it.

'Polly, Polly,' he blubbered, 'forgive me. But we thought you dead. We feared you had betrayed yourself to Galloping Jack and the other, and that they had slain you as well.'

Polly burst into laughter. 'Here is midsummer madness, Ned, to be sure. Do you think me such a clown as to betray myself to my enemies? And to boot, what is all this gallimaufry of Galloping Jack and the other murdering me?'

'It matters not,' said Will. 'Just so you be safe.' His face darkened with anger. 'But what make you in this wanton garb? Breeches on a lass? It is not seemly! Get you back into your skirts and corslets or whatever they are!'

But she caught openly admiring glances from the others. She knew that the masculine clothing, in some improbable way, made her more and not less feminine. She touched her father's shoulder affectionately – reassuringly – and walked past him to her grandmother. She kissed the withered old cheek.

'Thanks for guarding my secret, gran.'

The old woman grinned. 'They are fools, Polly, but your friends, for all that. Tell me now, lass, have you done with His Majesty's service?'

'Not yet.' Polly seized a flagon of ale and drank deeply. 'By the wounds of Jesu, but I was dry! Your claret wines are fine for the gentry but honest English ale is hard to beat!'

Whipt Ned drew close to her.

'Pray, Poll, what's afoot?'

'Gather round,' said Polly, hooking a rough stool towards her with her foot. She sat down on it, her long legs stretched out in front of her. 'Good friends, clapperdogeons, priggers, thieves and scoundrels, are you so far gone in wickedness, that you would not serve your king?'

They stared at her vacantly. What could she mean? Then Jem Hoskins spoke. 'Poll, we are no traitors here. Unwrap your mystery.'

'I want,' said Polly soberly, 'every man Jack in this cellar to mount guard throughout the length and breadth of this poor world of ours. There's treason brewing against King Charles

And I'll tell you whence it stems. From Galloping Jack and his lordship, the Earl of Kinnerton.

'Watch for them both. Follow them wherever they go. Listen to what they say. Let not their slightest lightest whisper escape your ears. Set your wives and children to work.

'The king has no guard at Whitehall like to you for keenness. Who can escape your eyes and ears? None! For you are part of London, you melt away – you vanish among the ruins and hovels. You are unseen, and thus none would suspect you.

'Find me these men, dear friends. Tell me what they say and what they plan against our sovereign lord the king!' She looked about.

Her audience moved uneasily. Finally Jem asked, 'But what are we to look for?'

'For evil,' Polly replied succinctly. 'For those, I doubt not, who would betray us all to the enemies of England. Now, Jem, you take three men and stay close to the riverside. Father Will, you choose a band of followers – not too many, mind – and spread them about St Paul's.' She pointed to one man after another as she rapped out her orders: 'You to keep a weather eye on *Fancy Anne*. You and you and you to the gates of London. You to the Royal Exchange. You to the Steelyard, and you to Temple Bar.'

She paused. 'Will you do it?'

There was a mumble of assent.

'Then start now. And report your findings to Whipt Ned here.'

As they clattered up the stairs to Bandyleg Lane, Ned stared at her in awe.

'What you want, Poll, shall be done if we can do it. But how should such poor folk as we serve the king better than his own men? Has he not armies and navies?'

'Yes,' Polly replied. 'But this is no battle that they can fight. This one must be fought in the dark, and only those who can see in the dark will win.'

CHAPTER VIII

TWO HOOKS FOR THREE FISHES

In the busy life of the River Thames, passing boatmen scarcely noticed that a new craft had joined their number – a tiny ramshackle skiff, barely riverworthy and long unpainted. It appeared each day at about sunrise just off Whitehall Palace's privy steps. Its owner would moor to a buoy, take up a rod and line and sit peacefully fishing, his body slumped on the thwarts, his battered hat tipped over his eyes. Nor did the regular boatmen notice that, at about the same time, a tall girl would appear on the palace's battlemented roof, glance down towards the fisherman and then, without a word or sign, vanish again.

Indeed, the last thing that either Whipt Ned, sitting in his leaky skiff, or Polly Fitch, high above, wanted was to be noticed. Ned had only one task: to be there, to drop his line overside, and seemingly to doze, lulled by the stream's easy motion. But were he to change the pattern, to drop two lines instead of one, Polly would be ready to act. For this was the signal that her darkling tatterdemalion army had picked up, among the ruins, the trail of the Earl of Kinnerton, Galloping Jack and Captain Pargiter.

Court gossips, their tongues busily wagging about the king's new wench, had not failed to observe that Polly was a strange new departure in royal courtesans. Morning after morning, to everyone's bewilderment, she and the king were seen to enter a small carriage, its windows curtained and free of all royal insignia, and to drive off in the direction of the burned areas. That Charles might find it amusing to conduct his amours in the confines of a carriage was unlikely, but just barely conceivable. But that he should, as he now did, have a third person ride along with them, made the entire affair bizarre.

Samuel Pepys, the omnipresent diarist, secretary of the Navy and habitué of the palace, whose inquisitive eyes missed little, wrote a baffled entry in his famous journal:

'Up betimes and to Whitehall, there to see the king set forth in a drab small carriage with but one horse, a coachman sans royal uniform and no postillion whatever. He was accompanied by the new female arrival of whom all speak (though they know no more than I) and also by Dr Christopher Wren. That the king beds her, there can surely be little doubt, and indeed my lady of Castlemaine's suspicions on this point are grown so mighty that she has been known to turn her back on Mistress Fitch in the Stone Gallery. But that Dr Wren with His Majesty shares the favours of this Venus – and in a small sorry carriage to boot – strains the imagination to breaking point. Discussed this with my wife who merely remarked that women were strange creatures (which indeed I knew myself). And so to bed.'

What the worthy Mr Pepys could have discovered with only the least bit of snooping was that Dr Wren owned the little coach, and that he had set up inside it a small folding table. On this, he spread out, as the three travelled, finely-drafted maps of the regions through which they rode. It was Polly's task to guide the pair – king and architect – through streets not only unknown to either of them, but not even familiar to the coachman. These were the small, sad and sordid streets in which she had grown up, crowded with the hovels of people she knew.

'There be,' Polly would say, 'eight living creatures in the cellar room in that dwelling, Your Majesty. Nineteen children were born there, of whom all but three died before a single year of their lives had passed.'

'Of the plague?' Charles might ask.

'No, sire, of a weakness of the bones, a blindness of the eyes, and ailments of chest and stomach.'

Dr Wren would note down the street's name.

'It must be at least the width of two carriages, sire.'

'Three, my good doctor. Od's fish, make it three. Do you agree, Polly?'

'Indeed, Your Majesty. Thus the sunshine can penetrate, and Your Majesty's subjects survive to manhood and womanhood.'

'Let us see to it, Dr Wren.'

And Christopher Wren would make a notation on his plan as the little carriage jounced off over the cobbles into the next filthy and obscure corner of King Charles's glorious capital in his glorious realm of seventeenth-century England.

Charles, though he was fully aware of the Whitehall tittle-tattle that linked his name with Polly's, and knew that many criticized the liaison as beneath him, shrugged it all off. Hypocritical moralizing was as much a part of court life as balls and masques. But he would have been most irritated if he could have peeped into the personal journal of the sanctimonious John Evelyn:

'The court is a scene of inexpressible profaneness and luxury, gaming and dissolution. In the king's glorious Banqueting House, I was witness to His Majesty toying with his latest concubine, whom all now call the Amazon, while a French boy sang love songs to the lute, and about twenty courtiers played at the cards with at least two thousand pounds in gold on the table before them. A pageant of the utmost vanity.'

To the censorious Evelyn, who had a far dirtier mind than Pepys, the so-called libertine, Charles was 'toying' if he so much as appeared in the same room with a comely woman, even though safely distant from her by some dozen un-adulterous paces. But on the particular night of which he wrote, Evelyn wasn't too wide of the mark. Charles, though listening to the French boy's *chansons d'amour*, was studying Polly's form as intently and minutely as if she were a prize filly up for sale at Newmarket: the proudly held head, the strong shoulders, the sleek thigh, now draped in softly clinging silk. She caught his eye; the thought of being assessed in this way amused her.

'Dam and sire undistinguished, Your Majesty,' she whispered behind her hand. 'Clears hurdles quite well but has yet to be tested on the flat.'

Charles roared with delight. Bart Ravenscroft turned, his smile quizzical, his eyes just faintly jealous.

'May I share the jest, my lord?'

'I was studying Poll as if she were a race horse, and she guessed it. Speaking of races, have I told you of the trick my cousin, Louis of France, tried to play on me?'

'His Gallic Majesty,' grumbled Clarendon, 'hasn't the wit for a trick.'

'Nor,' Kinnerton chimed in from the gaming table, 'the trick of wit.'

'You'll rhyme me that later, I'm sure,' Charles rejoined good humouredly. 'But I turned the trick against him. He sent me a soothsayer – a veritable reader of stars and omens – to riddle my fortune and to caution me that my only salvation was to support the French against the Dutch.'

Since England was then at war with both France and Holland, the suggestion was not only audacious, but, to the assembled courtiers, ludicrous.

Charles went on. 'I suspected that the old man was a charlatan and a humbug. So I took him to Newmarket, and to test him I asked him to predict the first three winners. He pursed his mouth like one forced to suck a lemon. Then he named three nags. I challenged him to wager on his own predictions, and he lost fifty sovereigns.' A broad smile lit the king's face. 'I sent a gift by him to Louis, and I told him that he would serve his royal master better if he were to hold my gift for him than his divining ball.'

'What sort of gift?' asked Polly innocently.

'A chamber pot. Poor Louis, he is so exceedingly, vain-gloriously royal that he cannot even pass water unless a servant holds the pot.' Laughter swept through the room. Charles, chuckling, slipped his arm around Polly's waist.

'But I was a dunce to compare you with a Newmarket filly. Better with the exquisite creations of my cousin Louis' gardener, André Lenôtre.'

'And which Versailles flower do I resemble, sire?'

'None, Poll. When my eye roams over you –' he dropped his voice to an intimate whisper, 'I am reminded not of flowers but of those swelling meads and soft curving grassy hillocks which Monsieur Lenôtre devises. Firm, yet yielding – inviting a man to cast his body down upon their contours, so cunningly designed, so softly formed.'

It was doubtless at this moment that the scandalized John Evelyn withdrew to complete his journal for the night.

Lady Castlemaine, watching from the gaming table, rose and swept across the room towards the king, her lovely body, swathed in a silver gown, cutting like a rapier through the press of people. Her face was white, her lips tightly-drawn. She sank in a curtsey.

Charles was apprehensive. 'My lady Castlemaine?'

'May I have Your Majesty's permission –'

He broke in. 'Anything, my dear Barbara. But will it not keep till morning? You look tired – a touch vapourish, perhaps? The room is so very hot.'

Barbara's pale cheeks flushed. In her mind she cursed her lover. He had guessed her intent and utterly spoiled her exit.

'Your Majesty is indeed perceptive, as always. I wished to ask your permission to withdraw.'

Charles's dark worldly face creased into a smile. There was mockery in his eyes.

'Indeed, Barbara, you have it freely. Late hours serve only to wilt so delicate a bloom as you.'

Barbara muttered spitefully, glancing at Polly, 'Some seem not to suffer.'

'In my own case,' Charles went on as though she hadn't spoken, 'it seems not to matter how little I rest. There is naught can make worse what nature already so lamely fashioned.

'Sleep well, my dear countess. Shall I dispatch one of my yeomen to guard your door and to see that you are not disturbed?'

'There is no need of that, sire.'

Charles extended his hand. Barbara knelt to kiss it and, as she did so, looked up boldly into his smiling eyes and hissed, 'God damn you, Charles!'

'He does, my dear countess from time to time, but we usually come to an understanding in the end.'

Barbara rose and retired, fury in her every movement.

The scene both amused and embarrassed Polly. She knew that she was no more than a temporary threat to Lady Castle-

94

maine. Even if Charles should urge her to remain in Whitehall, she would say him nay. To be one woman among many – even the king's – was not for Polly Fitch: her pride in herself was all she had. She had come to perform one duty; she had been sidetracked into another. When both were finished, she would go back to Bandyleg Lane. She had too much to do to engage in a feud with the *maîtresse en tître*. She asked the king if she too might be excused. Charles looked disappointed.

'Is my company so poor, Poll, that all my ladies wish to escape me?'

'Quite the contrary, as Your Majesty well knows. But in withdrawing from the field, Lady Castlemaine has set a good example. I would not appear to be the victor.'

'Well,' Charles mused, 'perhaps you are right.' He gestured to Ravenscroft, beckoning him over.

'Bart, will you see Mistress Fitch to her quarters?'

Bart bowed. 'A pleasure, sire.'

The pair withdrew. Charles's melancholy kindly gaze followed their tall forms as they passed from the hall. So young, so unweighted by care. He speculated on what sort of child their two strong, young bodies might produce. A lithe and forthright lad, perhaps, who in years to come would loyally serve an aging monarch. 'Od's fish,' he muttered to himself, 'the king is filled with self-pity tonight.' He took a peach from a majolica bowl and bit into the sweet moist flesh. 'I must banish these dour thoughts; they accord not with my nature.'

A courtier glided up.

'Your Majesty spoke?'

'A private dialogue only, between me and my lesser self.'

Baffled, the courtier bowed once more and retreated. Charles called him back.

'Sire?'

'Bid Chiffinch attend me.'

The man hastened away. As an antidote to self-pity, the king reflected wryly, the Stuarts usually turned either to war or to the arms of a woman. His current conflicts with the Dutch and the French were far off at sea, where he could not risk his life – not with the prospect of his brother James's succession.

One day James might well have to take his place, Charles reflected, but not, he hoped, before he had had time to smooth over the frictions that still existed in his recently restored kingdom. He often spoke of '*les sottises de mon frère*' – my brother's idiocies.

So, if war was an unattainable poultice for his melancholy, there was but one alternative.

Lady Castlemaine had lingered in the Privy Garden. The night air cooled her feverish temper, leaving only the chill of anger in its place. The flower-beds shone palely in the moonlight, almost as pale as the silver robe she wore. She stalked the paths like a ghost. Whence had she come, Barbara asked the empty night, this Fitch woman? This tall slut who had robbed her – she was sure of it – of the king's caresses?

She knew all too well that no shrewish ranting and railing could move the king. Reproaches only brought to his eyes that maddening glint of derision. Tears – so terrifying to other men – caused him only to turn away in fastidious distaste. If the attack could not be launched directly against Charles, then it must strike with all the fury of a grand lady rejected against the cause of her rejection.

Fitch woman, bitch woman! She paced back and forth, frustrated.

A flitting shadow darted swiftly from the direction of the Stone Gallery to the passage that led to the Banqueting House. Will Chiffinch! He would not leave his post near the king's bedchamber except by royal command. And for Charles to summon Chiffinch at this time of night, meant only one thing.

He was to be sent once again on the pimp's errand he had so often performed for his royal master. How many times, she mused bitterly, long after the candles had guttered in the great rooms of Whitehall, had he been sent thus to fetch her? How many times had she heard his soft scratching at the door and followed him through secret passages that only he and Charles knew to the great bedchamber overlooking the river? The scene was so familiar – the king in his nightshirt, surrounded by his dogs, sitting by his hearth – that she could recite the dialogue as if it had been written in a play:

'You were kind to come, Barbara. I could not sleep.'

'Your mind is so active, Charles. What thought disturbed you this time? Parliament? France? Spain? The Scots?'

'The thought of you, countess, alone in your gatehouse, a beautiful woman, unprotected in this wicked Whitehall of mine.'

'I am grateful for Your Majesty's concern.'

He was always like that – considerate, withholding his own desire. Other men hasted towards bed – she had known so many, been tumbled by so many. But Charles, the king, approached each episode, no matter how often it had been repeated, with the same, grave, diplomatic courtesy. He who might more easily than any other in the realm command a woman's body seemed only to be sueing for a kiss, like a rustic boy in his manhood's first midsummer.

But tonight it was not – she knew it – for her that Chiffinch would be dispatched. As she chewed this bitter cud of regret, Chiffinch reappeared, moving on silent feet. And the direction he took was towards Polly Fitch's quarters.

Lady Castlemaine bit her full lower lip. The volcanically violent rage that Charles so dreaded began to boil up within her. She determined on a desperate stratagem. Chiffinch, since he was performing his procurer's task in a distant part of the palace, would not be at hand to stay her from his master's privy rooms. Charles himself, she knew, was still in the Banqueting House, for his personal guard remained on duty outside.

She took the circuitous route through the palace's hidden passages, and ten minutes later settled herself, facing the door, in a deep, high-backed, heavily-carved chair within the bed-chamber she knew so well. She carefully arranged her full skirts, and, her face as grim with vengeance as that of an ancient Greek masque, she awaited Polly's arrival. She had made her plans heatedly; now, in solitary quietude, she reviewed them.

If Charles should come first, she would confront him directly: he must choose between Polly and herself. Despite everything, she felt confident that it would be she who would triumph. The king would not, for a brief new pleasure, for ever cut himself off from all the sensual joy that she bestowed. As for her own sexual infidelities, she knew it mattered not a fig to him, just so she avoid catching the pox and bringing it back to his bed. Adultery, after all, was the pattern of the court. Barbara doubted that there was one truly faithful wife in all of Whitehall, saving only that poor shrinking Queen Catherine who, for the empty gift of a crown, had undergone public humiliation greater almost than any queen in England's history.

Barbara repeated mentally, as if trying to convince herself, that her relationship with Charles had lasted long and went far deeper than casual gratification. And the children formed a mighty bond. Yes, the uncrowned queen of Whitehall was certain that against Mistress Fitch she would be the easy victor.

And if the wench were to arrive first? That was a lesser problem. She would simply dismiss the beggar maid – send her away. 'She would not dare defy me,' she said aloud. The spaniels whined in answer.

Barbara heard footsteps outside and the door inched open. Would it be Polly or Charles? She felt as if an iron band had whipped about her chest; she could scarcely breath.

The door opened further. Polly Fitch stood on the threshold.

Polly stared at the woman, seated in stately poise, with consternation and surprise. Surely Charles had not sent for them both! If he had, what did he have in mind? Some sort of truce between them?

Barbara Castlemaine spoke with cool, crisp authority. 'You have, no doubt, lost your way, girl. This is His Majesty's bed-chamber.'

'I have not, madame.' The 'girl' rankled, but Polly kept her head, closing the door firmly behind her. 'I am here by the king's express command. And you?'

There was no point in lying. 'I am not accustomed to being questioned. But, no, I am not here by His Majesty's command. Rather, for His Majesty's good. He is not to be pursued by every avaricious, pox-ridden, dirty slattern who manages, through what devious means I cannot guess, to insinuate herself into Whitehall. The king is, by nature, a kind and generous man, but his generosity is not to be imposed upon. Therefore, be gone.'

'I had thought,' Polly replied, 'that good manners and gentility were attributes of the gently born. I see that I was mistaken. Even in Bandyleg Lane, we use each other with consideration. Your upbringing, countess, was clearly deficient.'

Barbara sprang to her feet, her face drained of blood, her hands trembling.

'I have ordered you to leave. Obey me, or I will have you turned out like the common whore you are!'

'As for that, Lady Castlemaine,' Polly replied evenly, 'we are both whores – if whoredom means to give one's body in exchange for favours. Your whoring has been more successful than mine, if one is to judge by the jewels you wear. But then you are far older, and have had a longer time to practice your profession. Fear not, I shall catch you up.'

Barbara Castlemaine sprang towards Polly and seized her by the shoulders in a mad attempt to push her out of the room. She was no match for the younger, taller, stronger girl. Polly, never having been softened by luxury, was steel-muscled and lithe.

In an instant, she broke Barbara's grip, thrust her strong fingers through her foe's elaborate coiffure, twisted her head, and forced her to the floor. As she fell, Barbara clutched at Polly's low bodice, tearing it loose and leaving long red streaks where her sharp fingernails raked the firm skin of the bared bosom.

Polly cried out in pain, pulled Barbara up to her knees and launched a systematic programme of utter ruination. First she demolished the hairdress, already disarranged, so that the long auburn curls hung awry across Barbara's face. Then she ripped the silvery gown apart until the floor was covered with shining threads and glittering beads. And finally she seized a flagon of claret and poured it over the sobbing cursing face of the most famous royal courtesan of her day.

Her work completed, Polly stepped back, holding together

the gaping rent in her own bodice.

Throughout the brief battle the spaniels had cowered in a corner. They must have witnessed many curious encounters in that bedchamber, but surely none so bizarre as this!

As Barbara lay panting, unable to rise, one of the dogs ventured out. He walked towards her, his nose twitching with curiosity, and stood staring down at her. Then, with growing interest and appreciation, he began to lick away the splashes of claret from her face.

This was the moment the king chose to arrive. He took in the scene swiftly, but his face remained utterly impassive.

'I had intended earlier this evening,' he said at length in his thoughtful polite way, 'to present you two ladies to each other, since you are both so zealous in my interests. But I see that you have already met.'

He turned to the spaniel, who had abandoned Barbara, and stood wagging his tail before his master. 'Hannibal, what a bad dog you are to have tipped your master's claret over Countess Castlemaine. I can scarcely apologise enough, my dear countess, for this animal's abominable behaviour.'

Hannibal whined and sat up in front of Charles in the classic begging posture of all dogs. The king looked at him sternly. 'No, sir, down, I say, down. You shall not win me over so easily. You are dismissed from my favour for' – he hesitated – 'for an entire quarter of an hour.'

Barbara Castlemaine rose unsteadily to her feet, gathering about her the shreds of her ruined gown.

'And torn your dress too, has he, Barbara?' Charles went on. He returned to Hannibal. 'You are indeed a wicked beast. Half an hour then, and let me hear no whimper from you. To your corner, sir.'

Hannibal retreated, the worried expression that nature had given him, even more troubled and puzzled than usual.

'Your Majesty,' Barbara Castlemaine began, 'I am humbly –'

'Not at all, no apologies, my dear Barbara. A most unpleasant experience for you. You are excused. You may retire.'

He turned to Polly, 'Mistress Fitch, I had asked Will Chiffinch to escort you hither to discuss some new thoughts I have about St Paul's, but I find myself strangely weary. Another time will do as well.'

The two women curtseyed – Polly still clutching her bodice together, Barbara incongruous, in her tattered gown. Charles bowed and, as the pair backed out, he turned back to his dogs. Hannibal rushed over to him, his tail thrashing eagerly, his soft brown eyes alight with hope.

'Hannibal, you have behaved like a perfect gentleman, and you shall have an extra bone.'

The following dawn Whipt Ned rowed his skiff to his accustomed place beneath the palace walls. On the roof, Polly watched as he cumbrously tied up to his buoy, baited his hook and dropped his line into the stream. A single line only: Polly was disappointed. Still no news from Bandyleg Lane. She was about to turn away when she saw Ned reach down into the bottom of the craft, then straighten up, holding a second rod and line.

Deliberately he baited the hook, his head bent low over his task. Then he glanced upward towards the battlements and casually dropped it overside. *Two* lines now curved to the pull of the tide.

So, Polly sighed with relief, at last someone among her friends had got on to the trail of the conspirators. But of which one? Kinnerton, Galloping Jack, Captain Pargiter? Or all three?

As she descended to the courtyard, she wondered if her vigil might be almost over. If it were – if the information she sought was now to hand – she had only to report her findings to the king. Then, if he had no further need of her – and why should he? – she would return to her old life.

And Barbara, Countess of Castlemaine, would have Charles to herself again. It was just as well. Though the king had been exquisitely polite the night before, he could scarcely have relished the spectacle of two ladies of his court brawling like fishwives in his bedchamber.

She spent the day in her quarters, withdrawn as a nun. As dark fell, she summoned one of the newly-invented hackney

carriages and drove eastward. At the bridge over the Fleet
River she alighted and paid the coachman. A few minutes later
she was descending the worn familiar steps that led to Granny
Fitch's kitchen.

CHAPTER IX

FORMULA FOR TREASON

Ned rose from his seat by the hearth when he saw Polly. He had with him a lad of about fourteen whom she had never seen before. The boy's face was gaunt, and unruly blond hair hung in wisps over his forehead. He wore a leather apron.

'Poll, you come in the tick of time. This is Hal Townsend. The potboy at the Three Graces.'

Hal gave an awkward bob of his head and looked embarrassed.

'Hal, tell Mistress Fitch what you just told me.'

The boy rubbed his hands together nervously and cleared his throat. Polly, wearing the least handsome of her Whitehall dresses, was still, in his eyes, a grand and overwhelming lady.

Polly calmed him. 'Don't be afeard, Hal. Just speak out.'

The boy gulped. 'Yes, missus. Well, like Whipt Ned asked me, I kept my eye on the comin's and goin's at the Graces. I han't seen nobody of what I was to watch for – he give me fourpence did Mr Ned – and then yesterday I heard the master – that's the landlord of the Graces – give orders to prepare the upstairs room for some gennelmun as was comin' tonight.

'I made up the fire myself and was told off to be potboy to the gennelmun, and soon after one of 'em come. And I hears me master call him Lord – I couldn't catch the name, but it was sommat sounds like 'Kinnen' – or 'Kinton', mayhap.

'So I brings him a pot of clarey wine – the best in the house – and he says, 'Bring three goblets, boy.' So I knows as there's others coming. An' I goes down to fetch the goblets, and outside I hears a horse stampin' and snortin'.'

He cut his narrative off, suddenly hesitant, apprehensive.

Ned growled, 'Well, get on with it, lad.'

'Hal,' Polly asked, 'whose horse was it?'

'I didn't see it, missus. But I saw the man what owned it when he come in.' His eyes popped and his voice shook. 'Gallopin' Jack.'

Poll asked sharply, 'Hal, are they there now?'

'Oh, yes, missus. In the upstairs room.'

'Just the two?'

The gormless boy nodded. 'But there's bound to be another. He asked for three goblets, didn't he?'

Ned caught Polly's eye.

'Who'd be the third man, think you, Poll?'

'Pargiter, of a surety. The skipper of *Fancy Anne*.'

Ned reached into his pocket, took out a second fourpenny piece, and tossed it beguilingly up and down in his hand.

'Now pay attention, Hal. You must go back as though nothing had happened.'

'Yes, master Ned.'

'And listen, lad – this is important – you must find some way that we can hear what they say in the room. Is there a place we can hide?'

Hal scratched his blond head.

'You and the missus both?'

Ned nodded.

'There's a little room next door with a hatch through the wall to where the gennelmun be. It's what I passes drink through when it's wanted.'

'And,' Whipt Ned asked, 'you can make out their words?'

The potboy nodded.

'But if they tell you to close the hatch, what then?'

'You can hear fine, even then.'

'How so?' Polly asked.

Hal grinned. 'Didn't I put a hole in it myself by the lower edge last Michaelmas?'

'A hole? But sure they can see it from the other side!'

Hal shook his head. His grin broadened. 'They never do, Master Ned. I drilled it there with a little bore, so I could watch when they takes their doxies up. Such kissin' and cuddlin' and nuzzlin' and undoin' of laces and buttons – oh my!' He reddened in embarrassment. 'Savin' your presence, missus!'

Polly spoke curtly: 'Can you get us into the little room? So nobody sees us come or go?'

'Ye-e-s,' Hal replied doubtfully. 'But it's a right risk, missus.

If I was caught, my master'd thump me and turn me out.'

Whipt Ned held up the fourpenny bit. The boy's eyes glistened.

'I'll do it. But you mun be quiet as mice.'

'We will,' Polly assured him. 'But come! We must leave at once.'

They climbed to the potboy's serving place, a tiny heavily-panelled chamber, by way of a rear entrance to the Three Graces. The hatch was closed, but as Hal had promised, they could clearly hear the voices from next door. They arrived just as Pargiter entered the other room. Kinnerton greeted him.

'Good evening, captain.'

'Evenin', my lord,' Pargiter replied gruffly. There was the liquid splash of wine being poured, and again Pargiter's voice: 'Thankee kindly, my lord.'

Then came a thump, followed by the jingling clink of metal.

'Money,' Polly mouthed voicelessly. Ned nodded.

Galloping Jack asked, 'Is that it, Pargiter?'

'Aye, his lordship's importation from Holland. Five thousand pounds in good Dutch gold. As guaranteed by our friends in the Hague, gentlemen. Will you count it?'

Galloping Jack spoke. 'No need. If the sum be short by so much as a florin, I've a little sharp-edged friend as loves the taste of a sailor's blood. You'll not be wanting to slake that thirst, now will you, captain?'

'Nay, Jack,' stammered Pargiter with a false show of joviality. 'You know me better than that. In the three years since we first met in the Netherlands and did our little business with the rum, have I ever played you false?'

'Enough,' Kinnerton interposed sharply. 'You're both of you scoundrels and smugglers and rogues. And well I know it, but I've no choice. When the thing's done, is *Fancy Anne* ready to sail?'

'We lie with our hawser up and down, my lord, and can slip our cable as soon as you've got him aboard.'

'Three nights from now, a darkened coach will arrive at the ship's side. I'll want none of your crew about the ladder –

none, mind! – to spy on what's brought aboard!'

'They'll be in the tops, sir, ready to unfurl the sails –'

'Yes, yes.'

'But sir, it won't do to be late. The tide turns at eleven and we must catch the ebb for a quick departure.'

'What if we're boarded in the Downs by the guards?'

'Why should we be? They all know *Fancy Anne*. Outward bound for the slaving coasts with a load of trade goods, then from Africa over to Jamaica with the slaves and home again with sugar and spices. There'll be nothing to show this trip's any different. Whistle for a fair wind down the Channel, and we'll drop old England below our horizon in the morning. Then naught but open water between us and the Isles of Cape Verd.'

'Deep water,' mused Galloping Jack.

'Aye, deep enough to swallow –'

'Yes,' Kinnerton interrupted, 'to swallow anything it might be in our interest for you to put overside on a dark night.'

A heavy silence filled the unseen room. Polly and Ned glanced at each other. Hal leaned against the wall, his tow hair in his eyes, his slack mouth hanging open in idiotic boredom. Kinnerton called, 'Boy, boy, more wine!'

Hal sprang to attention, thrust the two listeners away from the hatch, and opened it.

'Yes, my lord. At once, my lord.' He reached through the opening for the wine jug, jogged across the tiny room, turned the tap of a small dark barrel, and hastened back to the hatch. 'Here, my lord.'

Kinnerton took the jug.

'Now shut that thing.'

'Yes, my lord.'

Hal closed the hatch.

'Come, Jack,' Kinnerton said, 'pour bumpers all round.'

'Your good health, my lord.' That was Pargiter. 'And death to those who oppose us!'

Galloping Jack chimed in, 'And good luck to the Protestant House of Orange, for them's the ones that pays.'

'Of Stuart, surely,' said Pargiter. 'Once Monmouth's on the

106

throne –'

'He will be,' remarked Kinnerton, 'no more than a creature of the princes of the Low Countries. It's their gold, and it is their tune that shall be danced to. Let the two brothers be but gone – and York will prove no trouble for he's a coward, and will take to his heels for Catholic France – then it's King Monmouth on the throne and Billy Orange to pull the strings behind it.'

'Be that as it may,' observed Galloping Jack, 'I care little, as your lordship knows, for politics. It's the cash I want – cash and a fresh start anywhere outside this troubled land.'

'And you shall have it,' Kinnerton replied. 'After the deed is done this hour three nights.'

'Fret not!' Jack said. 'We have the gold, we have the ship, we have the plan.'

'Aye, but the tiger's not yet dead. Nor drowned, Jack. And while he lives, his claws are sharp. It's fools like you – thinking things are done before they're begun – that keep such men as he on the throne, and the threat of the Pope's long skinny hand still hanging over England.'

'Have no fear,' said Pargiter. 'What is needful, we will see to. Then hey for King Jemmie and the coasts of Africa!'

'She sprang at me, Charles.' Barbara Castlemaine struggled to keep her voice under control. 'I tell you, she attacked me! Like a wildcat from the jungle! You saw my gown! You saw my hair!'

Charles surveyed the beautiful termagant thoughtfully, with a slight feeling of hopelessness. What an unleashed force of nature Barbara was – so fascinating, so stylish, so lacking in restraint. He considered bringing the interview to an end with the best weapon at his command, withdrawal into the royal hauteur. At times, this came naturally to him. But not now.

Grudgingly, he could see Barbara's point of view. And yet, he argued with himself, what right had she to deny him the choice of any female he wished? He knew that he was self-indulgent. But, by way of excuse, had he not the endless cares of state upon his shoulders?

Earlier the previous evening he had been closeted with Samuel Pepys, perusing the naval accounts. Unless Parliament would agree to larger sums for ships, he would have to lay the fleet up for the winter. In the face of the relentless naval pressure by the damned Dutch, this was suicide. Charles loved the navy; the thought of its skulking within harbour while the war vessels of the Low Countries lorded it over the narrow seas between England and the Continent, sickened and dismayed him. Not since Sir Francis Drake defeated the Spanish Armada nearly a century earlier had England willingly relinquished control of the English Channel.

But Parliament, as always, was defying him over money. Caught between their parsimony and the quiet chilling financial facts marshalled by that clever, soft-spoken and diplomatic Samuel Pepys, Charles had felt trapped. Hence, he had sought the only cure for melancholy he knew. And Barbara Castlemaine had transferred his hoped-for rendezvous into a slatternly imbroglio.

'You had no business in my bedchamber, Babs,' he pointed out logically. 'I did not send for you.'

'I know that well enough. But sometimes, my dear lord, you need protection from yourself. What can a king want with a gutter slut like the Fitch wench?'

'Her instincts,' Charles countered, 'are far less sluttish than you might imagine.'

'You'll be making her out an angel next. Charles, you're changing. You're developing a low taste for strumpets. I've watched you at the theatre with your eyes on those actresses. And God knows what their origins may be. They say that the new one, Eleanor Gwyn, is the daughter of a brothel keeper!'

'Mayhap, mayhap. But still, her art amuses me, this Mistress Gwyn. She appears to have a merry way with her, a pert, delightful little person, as English as strawberries and cream.' He spoke partly out of devilment, to annoy Lady Castlemaine, but partly because he had thought this thought before. From his royal box, he had admired Nell Gwyn, as so many did, and had allowed his thoughts to encompass a possible meeting. So far, however, he had taken no step in that direction.

'Or as English as horse dung in the roadway.' Barbara's eyes flashed dangerously. 'Such women degrade kings, sire. Have you forgotten Lucy Walter?'

'You speak, Barbara,' Charles replied with a dignity to which there was a sudden edge of chill, 'of matters that are no concern of yours. Lucy, indeed, became an embarrassment at the end, poor lass. But she was kind to me when I needed kindness. A lad, penniless, exiled, with a father condemned to the scaffold.'

'She took advantage of your innocence. She knew full well that you were the heir apparent – that one day you might sit on the throne.'

'Then, if that were so, Barbara, Lucy and I took mutual advantage of each other. And I have much to thank her for; she gave me my first and most beloved son.'

'Who hates you with all his heart!'

'Nay, that he does not. He loves me. But his road is difficult. To be a king's first-born, with no hope ever of becoming king – and yet to have kingly juices coursing through his body. And immortal longings, as Cleopatra says, racing through his mind and making his heart swell. I know Jemmie's failings, Barbara. But he does not hate his father. He would be loyal with his dying breath!'

Barbara saw from the gravity of Charles's words that she had gone too far.

'May Your Majesty's faith be justified,' she said quietly.

'Come, then, Barbara, one kiss and we must part. Let us kiss, as true lovers should, upon a note of kindness and of understanding. I am sorry your dress was torn, but I'll furnish you another.'

Barbara Castlemaine kissed the full-lipped, appealing mouth. She felt herself soften. Then the humiliation of her battle with Polly sprang vividly to mind and she dared again to speak.

'Indeed, let us be true lovers, dear one,' she whispered. 'And you will promise me to banish this woman from Whitehall?'

'Nay, I did not say that.'

'Then,' Barbara went on, still in a gentle voice, 'there can be no place at your court for poor Barbara Castlemaine. You have a king's pride, Charles, but I have a woman's.'

'You would leave the palace?'

'I would have but little choice, sire.'

Charles almost blurted out, 'Leave then and be damned.' But he curbed his anger. Barbara had strong influence over several of his ministers. He knew that she pulled strings, granted favours, gave gifts. An open rupture could bring her partisans rushing fervently to her side, lined up staunchly against him.

And with London agog with tales of arson and espionage, any kind of division in his own household could only weaken his position *vis-à-vis* his opponents in Parliament, and imperil even further his chances of getting the money he needed to keep his navy afloat. He must not only be master of his personal affairs, but be seen to be master by all.

'Very well, Barbara, you hold a pistol at my heart. I surrender.'

'And she, Charles my own, has twisted a dagger in mine.'

Poor Polly, he thought. So unaware of the poison in this accursed snakepit called Whitehall, so innocent of guile. He would reward her well. And never forget the girl who had saved his life and then taught him how his subjects lived.

There were voices outside the chamber. Then a knock. It was Chiffinch.

'Your Majesty, Mistress Fitch is here. She asks audience.'

Charles caught Barbara's eye.

'I am otherwise occupied, Chiffinch. Send her away.' He paused, and added, 'But gently, man, gently.'

Chiffinch hesitated, his hand on the door. Something in the king's tone made him sense that this was not a firm order.

How extraordinarily unfortunate, Charles thought to himself. Why did fate time things so awkwardly? He could be hard, cynical and merciless. What he could not easily be was discourteous.

There had been, during his exile, an unfortunate contretemps with the landlord of a Belgian inn, some small disagreement over the cost of rooms and food. The innkeeper had been difficult when he brought the reckoning, and Charles, penniless and ashamed, had flared up in response to the man's rudeness with an unseemly rudeness of his own. His boorish ill manners had been more fit for a travelling pedlar than for a king. The memory rankled even now. He had vowed never again to be less than royal in his treatment of others.

How could he brusquely dismiss one to whom he owed so much? If he sent Polly away now, he must promise her an audience later. But to hear him say this to Will Chiffinch would set Barbara's blood boiling again.

Chiffinch eased the way for him. 'My lord, she is not alone.'

'Who accompanies her?'

'Your Majesty's Gentleman of the Bedchamber, Master Ravenscroft.'

Charles racked his memory. Had he arranged a meeting – again to talk of London's meanest corners? Mayhap Polly was come not to speak again of last night, or to beg for another rendezvous, but truly on royal business.

Barbara impatiently took charge.

'You heard His Majesty when you entered, Chiffinch. The king is otherwise occupied.'

Her intervention flicked Charles on the raw. 'I pray you, my lady, allow me to arrange my affairs in my own way.'

'But sire, you said –'

'I shall receive them, Chiffinch.'

'Very good, Your Majesty.'

Chiffinch withdrew. Barbara turned on Charles.

'Your Majesty gives and then withdraws the gift. Is it not the attribute of kings that their plighted word may be trusted as a bond?'

'She comes not to bed with me, Lady Castlemaine. Pray you, wait and see the outcome for yourself.'

Chiffinch reopened the door, bowing, 'Mistress Fitch, my lord, and Master Ravenscroft.'

Both made their reverences. Polly flushed, embarrassed and dismayed at coming face to face with Lady Castlemaine. She withdrew to one side of the door to allow her to pass. But Barbara stood firm.

'Our business, sire,' Bart said humbly, 'is private.'

Barbara tried to will words into Charles's mouth. She

appeared calm as she stared at the king with masque-like poise; only the flicking of her fingers revealed her agitation. She concentrated hard: Order Master Ravenscroft to go, and to return with his 'private business' later – and alone.

Charles, however, welcomed his visitors with a smile.

'You may speak freely, both of you. Nothing is so private that my Lady Castlemaine may not hear.'

A chill smile touched Barbara's lips. This was indeed a royal rebuff to the beggar-maid from Bandyleg Lane.

'As Your Majesty desires,' said Bart. 'Yet the matter is of some delicacy, and may not interest her ladyship.'

'That which is of consequence to my lord the king,' Barbara replied coldly, 'can never fail to concern his faithful servant.'

Polly stepped towards Charles apologetically, almost timidly.

'It is your life, sire, we come to speak of. Your life and your death.'

'My death, Polly? Well, let that come when it will, it is a debt one owes to God. I shall find means to pay it.'

'But not,' said Ravenscroft, 'before 'tis due.'

'Od's fish no, Bart. Until then, life is sweet. But come, who is it then that would demand payment before the allotted time?'

Both Bart and Polly hesitated.

'Come,' the king repeated, 'who wants my life? And why?'

'My liege,' Polly replied finally, ' 'tis the Earl of Kinnerton.'

'Kinnerton?' the king laughed. 'Nay, surely not! He's a mere rhymester. A poet, with a sharp wit only. Not a poignard. Whom would he have left to annoy with his scurrilous verses, were I gone?'

He chuckled again. 'What say you, my Lady Castlemaine? Does Kinnerton thirst for our royal blood? You know the man. You hate each other with such mutuality, that surely you are the best of friends and understand each other well!'

Barbara Castlemaine did not laugh, nor even smile in return.

'I have never known him, sire, to engage in anything truly evil – only malicious.' She paused. 'Yet, mayhap you would do well to listen further.'

It was unbelievable to Polly that Barbara Castlemaine, her sworn enemy, should be willing to give ear to her!

'All right,' Charles replied. 'Then, Mistress Fitch, I am listening. Weave me your tale, just so it be true – and not one of a cock and a bull.'

Polly marshalled her thoughts, then recounted the details – the origins of her suspicions, and of Whipt Ned's; Mark Lampson's murder; the visit to *Fancy Anne*. But when it came to what she and Ned had overheard in the upstairs room at the Three Graces, her tongue balked. She could not force herself to mention James, Duke of Monmouth. Barbara's eyes sharpened.

'If I may speak, Your Majesty.'

'Indeed, Barbara, proceed.'

'This,' said Lady Castlemaine, 'is a strange tale, with slave ships and highwaymen and mysterious gold from the Low Countries and a plan to abduct Your Majesty. But there is one link missing a – a gap in the tale, methinks.'

'And that is – ?'

'Mistress Fitch,' said Barbara Castlemaine, 'did not your conspirators name the one they would enthrone in the king's stead? Some member of the Dutch royal house, perchance? Some rebel from Scotland?'

Polly looked for help to Bart Ravenscroft. He divined her distress.

'Your Majesty,' said Bart, 'Mistress Fitch does not wish to name the name for fear of –' he cast about for the right word, 'of vexing you.'

'Vexation,' Charles replied wearily, 'that is nothing new to me. Speak out, Polly. Who is my successor to be, once I am drowned full fathom five in African waters?'

'My lord,' Polly answered in a low tone, 'it is to be Your Majesty's son, the Duke of Monmouth.'

'I said it to you, Charles,' Barbara burst out, 'not ten minutes since.'

'And have you,' Charles asked Polly, 'any reason to believe that the duke knows aught of this conspiracy?'

'No, my lord, I have not. I neither saw him with these men,

nor did any of them say he was privy to the plan.'

'I knew it!' Charles's shout was triumphant. 'There is nothing to fear then! For once they bring their ugly schemes to Jemmie, my son will give them short shrift. He is my blood, the child of my first love!'

'And think you, sire,' Barbara asked quietly, 'that Kinnerton and the rest would go so far – that indeed the Dutch would send gold – without assurance of the duke's complicity?'

'Kinnerton,' Charles replied, laughing in his sudden relief, 'is mad enough to do anything. He breathes plots and breakfasts on conspiracies. They amuse him. They are his hobbies, as mine are tennis and horses. As for his colleagues, they're naught but sturdy rogues. They have no more political wisdom in their empty noddles among them all than there is philosophy in a hen's egg!'

'What of the Dutch gold?' Barbara persisted.

'Five thousand? A paltry sum. Why should not our Dutch friends venture it in the hope of causing just enough disturbance in this country to cripple our efforts at sea? Be assured, let but this matter once come out, and there'll be racing and chasing after plotters from Whitehall to the Tyne. They merely fish in troubled waters. That is all.'

He turned to Polly. 'I thank you for your zealousness, Mistress Fitch. I pray you, though, be not alarmed. The king of England is threatened twice a day, and thrice on Sundays!'

'But my lord –' This from Bart.

Charles waved him aside. 'Go to, lad, go to! I'll pull Kinnerton's ears for him one of these days. And that will end your mysteries. Look you, the people love me, my son loves me. And my guards are as stalwart as a wall of rock.'

His voice softened as he realized that, for all his own *bon-homie*, his young aide looked as worried as ever. 'I thank you for your concern, Bart. With all my heart. And you too, Mistress Fitch.' He was genuinely touched. He feared he might soon sound maudlin. Quickly, he changed the subject. 'Now I must meet with my council.'

Bart, Polly and Barbara Castlemaine backed out of the chamber.

Polly felt deflated. The king's reaction to her warning had been so totally different from what she had expected. Well, he was no doubt right. She had meddled in matters beyond her limited knowledge of the world. Like an inexperienced swimmer she had ventured into waters too deep. Her cheeks burned with chagrin as she moved along the corridor towards the Stone Gallery.

Then she felt a touch on her arm. It was Barbara Castlemaine.

'Madame,' said Barbara, 'we are enemies and I swear shall remain so until you leave Whitehall. But this I will say. I put credence in your story.'

'Thank you, my lady,' Polly replied.

'The king,' Barbara went on, 'is ever reluctant to believe what does not please him. If he refuses to listen, there is one who will. Like you, he is my enemy and hates me for my influence over His Majesty. But he remains the wisest man in London. Will you allow me to take you to him?'

'To whomever you advise,' said Polly.

'Then together we shall see the Earl of Clarendon. He will be at the council now. But later, will you tell your tale again?'

'Why do *you* believe me,' Polly asked simply, 'when the king laughs me to scorn?'

'Because you named the Duke of Monmouth. And Jemmie is a viper in the king's bosom. He would envenom Charles in an instant, if it would put a crown upon his head!'

CHAPTER X

SLAVE DECK

Grizzled little Clarendon sat behind a long oak table, with his back to the windows that overhung the Privy Gardens. It was a handsome room, opening off the Stone Gallery. Its walls were lined with heavily-bound books, mostly histories. On the table lay a pile of manuscript in Clarendon's neat crabbed hand, a pot of ink, several quill pens, a knife to sharpen their points, a box of sand to blot the wet ink and a huge outspread map. It showed the east coast of England, the Channel and the shores of France and the Low Countries.

'His Majesty,' said Clarendon, having heard Polly out carefully, 'is a true-born Stuart in every way. They have all been alike – and I have studied their characters back to the first of them.

'They are ruled by their hearts and their lusts. There is enormous generosity in their natures, and they cannot bring themselves to believe ill of any man or woman until events force the truth upon them.

'I have known the king since his boyhood, and never, even in the worst of times, have I seen him play the pessimist. It is because he is himself hopeful – a trait that is only partly subdued by a thin cover of cynicism – that he is slow to accept the evil intentions of others.

'He was a lad filled with optimism when he rode into battle at Worcester. He believed absolutely that, since ordinary people would fight beside him, the royal cause against Oliver Cromwell was just and would triumph. He had faith that they would place this cause above their own immediate self-interest. Well, he learned better when he saw his army crumble as Cromwell's men stormed the city at push of pike, and he himself was driven into exile. A bitter lesson, but salutary. Yet even in his years of wandering, he clung to the tattered threads of hope.

'This time, the enemy is less obvious. Now it lurks not only within his own kingdom and his own court, but even within the small and intimate circle of the very blood royal.

'How can a man who is himself without viciousness believe that his own son would strike a dagger into his back? And yet in the annals of kingship, this has happened many many times before.'

Bart Ravenscroft watched the old courtier's scholarly features intently. Lady Castlemaine stared beyond Clarendon's shoulder to where the afternoon sun slanted across the trees in the garden. How well, she thought, he understood Charles. Polly leaned forward in her chair, fascinated at this new insight into a man she knew only as lover and master.

'Then, my Lord Clarendon,' said the Countess of Castlemaine, still keeping her eyes on the sunlit world beyond the tall windows, 'I understand it that you take Mistress Fitch's warning more seriously than does the king?'

Clarendon steepled his wrinkled forefingers.

'It is not, of a certainty, a mere tale of a cock and a bull, as the king implied. For everything in it fits with what I know, and with what the king might know just as well, were he only capable of facing facts. Oh, he does face them eventually, but too late.

'The Dutch are at our throats. My lord of Kinnerton, as I happen to be aware, has certain private financial problems to solve.

'Young Monmouth believes himself to be not a bastard – he has, indeed, convinced himself that this is so – but the son of a holy union between His Majesty and Lucy Walter. He is also a Stuart, remember, and has had this dinned into his ears by the king's enemies. Stuart-wise, he chooses to take as true that which is most pleasant to hear, and to reject what he does not like.

'As for the slave ship, this *Fancy Anne*, what better way to maintain contact between London and the Dutch coast? We often send trade goods to Guinea from the Continent, as well as from this country. Any errands the vessel might have across the Channel would go unnoticed, as would the daily voyages of ships bearing coals hither from Newcastle.

'Which leaves us only Pargiter and the rogue, Galloping Jack. Plots cannot be plotted without fellows such as these to undertake the direst and most evil roles. Their employment is natural enough.'

'How can the king be convinced, sir?' Bart asked.

'That indeed, young man,' Clarendon replied in his slow, schoolmasterly way, 'is the next question to which I was about to address myself.'

Barbara withdrew her gaze from the garden. 'Cannot you, my lord, speak to His Majesty yourself?'

The grave face of Lord Clarendon broke into a rueful smile.

'As your ladyship is aware, there was a time when I might indeed have done so, and the king would have listened. But those days are gone and my influence, like that of Cardinal Wolsey over Harry the Eighth, has been whistled down the wind. The king finds me tiresome now, and my advice that of a garrulous old man. He stays from banishing me only for a slight sweetening of remorse that eases the bitterness of his exasperation with me.'

'I know. I'm sorry, my lord, I know.'

Her sympathetic tone was out of character for Barbara Castlemaine. Clarendon's words had been in part a reproof to her. His descent from favour was due largely to her, because of his unflagging and savage opposition to her influence over the king, and of his loyalty to Queen Catherine.

Although Barbara would always oppose him, whenever he seemed to stand in her way, she knew that, once he was gone, there would be a vacuum among the king's advisers which Charles would find it hard and dangerous to fill.

'No.' Clarendon shook his head. 'The old dog may bark, but the master no longer harkeneth.' He had a habit of slipping into the older forms of Elizabethan English from time to time. The informality of Restoration London had come too late in his life for him to accept it willingly or, indeed, at all.

'I see before me,' he went on, 'three young favourites. I can advise you, but I cannot bear your warnings to King Charles.'

'Then what is your advice?' Polly asked.

'I reply as I must, as a lawyer, bred and trained. Before a charge is made, there must be substantial evidence. You must ascertain explicitly what these people mean to do, how, where and when. You must surprise them in some act so flagrantly treasonable as to convince your judge and your jury – both, in this instance, combined in the king's royal person.

'I fear that to gather together all the facts that are needful may prove a perilous adventure. Your lives may be in danger – the life of Mistress Fitch in particular. Nonetheless, I have no choice but to council you thus.

'At whatever risk, assemble your evidence and then present your case.'

Bart glanced towards Polly. Clarendon was right, of course. There was indeed a risk, and Polly was the one likely to suffer.

Clarendon divined his thoughts.

'Mistress Fitch, loyalty to one's sovereign does not demand the putting of one's hand into the embers for his sake. You have warned him, and he has rejected your warning. You may, with a clear conscience, now withdraw from the whole affair.'

Polly straightened in her chair, her blue eyes fixed intently on Clarendon as she weighed his every word.

He continued. 'But, Mistress Fitch, should you choose to go on, then you must see the business through, no matter what the danger! It is the king's Majesty that stands in jeopardy. This is harsh – and you are young and beautiful. Yet may I repeat some words to you which I addressed many years ago to a courtier when we were all in exile? When we had scarce a shilling to divide among us.

'I said then, "I know of no other counsel to give you than that which, by the Grace of God, I intend to follow myself, which is to submit to God's pleasure and judgement upon me, and to starve really and literally rather than bow to rogues."'

He jolted himself back to the present. 'We are set about with evil. I would that it were as easy to cure it as to lament it.'

'Catherine,' said Charles, surveying the sweet, wan face of his queen, 'I want you to leave Whitehall for a while.'

'Leave Whitehall?' Catherine's big dark eyes widened. She

knew that, because of her religion and her barrenness, she was something of a liability to her husband – even a weapon in the hands of his enemies. 'Leave Whitehall?' She gasped. 'Not – not, for ever?'

He held her chin in his hand and looked down at her with real affection.

'No. Of course not, my dear. Only for a few days. Perhaps a little longer.'

Clarendon had been right about Charles's inherent optimism, but he did not realize that the king's trust that things would always right themselves in the end went only so far as his own well-being was concerned. Charles had interpreted Polly's warning in a way that neither she nor Bart had anticipated. The threat, he feared, was not to his person but to the queen's. And, in his strange amoral way, he loved Catherine dearly.

Once when she was ill he had sat at her bedside night after night alone, dismissing her ladies, bathing her and changing her linen himself. And he had prayed for her life. Many years later, on his own deathbed, he was to beg her forgiveness for his treatment of her during their long unsatisfactory marriage.

'But why should I go?'

'If I say that it is my wish, is that not enough?'

'Do you command me?'

'Nay, love, I do not command my sweet Catherine. I ask it.'

Catherine, with quick Mediterranean apprehension, leaped to the right conclusion. Where a lesser woman might have supposed he wanted the field clear in London for some new romance, she sensed a graver reason.

'You are in danger, Charles. Is that it?'

He shrugged. 'I'm always in danger. That is –' he paused, 'I mean, all kings are in danger. Peril and crown walk hand in hand. But you know that as well as I do.'

'The Dutch!' Catherine exclaimed. 'You fear an attack on London by the Dutch?'

'No greater fear than usual.'

'Unless you command me, Charles, I shall not stir from Whitehall – not without being certain of your safety. It ill befits a queen to leave her lord to face danger alone.'

How instinctively a regal, thought Charles, was this woman he had married. The images of his mistresses flitted through his mind. Which, amongst that garden of beautiful blooms, would stand up to the wintry blast of peril? But Catherine, neglected and so often humiliated, was made of different stuff.

'Divorce her,' his counsellors had often advised him. 'Marry again and beget an heir.' How little they knew the king they were dealing with, and the consort he had chosen. In that moment, more than at any other since their wedding, Charles and Catherine were truly man and wife.

'Very well,' said Charles. He sat beside her and took her hand in his. She smiled shyly, lowering her eyes with the same modest girlishness she had shown when the king first called her 'My Lady and Wife' in Portsmouth five years earlier. She adored his touch, but it had become so sadly unfamiliar to her.

'I have had intelligence,' said Charles, 'of a plot – it may be nothing, but it may have some substance in it – supposedly aimed at me. I fear, Catherine, that I am not the target, but rather you.'

'Or both of us?'

'Unlikely. Should I die, my brave foolish brother would succeed me. He is disliked – oh, my dear, to have to say this again to you – because many believe him to be a Catholic. This, the land will not accept. There would be riots, battles – possibly even another revolution and some new Cromwell within a few months. So you see, the threat of James II on the throne is by far the best protection possible for Charles II.

'But you, Catherine, are vulnerable.' He sighed. 'You know all too well the reasons why. And I must have my hands free if these rogues strike.

'I should like you to go to Windsor Castle; there you will be safe. But you must go secretly. We will give it out that you are ill and are confined to bed for several days. Thus the plotters – should they indeed exist – will, if they come in search of you here, find only me awaiting them.'

'Then you will be in peril!'

'Only the unprepared are in peril.' He drew her dark delicate face towards his. 'There will be a coach tonight ready to take you to Windsor.'

So, Catherine thought, he has already made all the necessary arrangements. This was typical of Charles – to disguise a command as a wish, a *fait accompli* as a mere suggestion. She closed her eyes in acquiescence. Suddenly she felt his lips on her mouth. She trembled at the unexpected embrace. He released her, and she turned away so that he would not see the tears.

'Very well, Charles. I shall be ready.'

A second later he was gone, her last glimpse of him, his broad shoulders disappearing through the door.

Charles walked with a spring in his step across the Privy Garden towards King Street, his courtiers falling back respectfully to make way. A spaniel trotted at his side. Now that Catherine was safe, he had but one other task.

On the far side of King Street, he entered the Duke of Monmouth's suite. A servant, standing at the door to his son's bedchamber, stammered in surprise.

'Your Majesty –?'

'Is his grace within?'

'The duke? No, Your Majesty. He has left the palace.'

'Where has he gone?'

'To Newmarket as I believe, sire. And then to Leicester, to hunt.'

Charles felt an enormous lightening of his heart. He had intended to send Monmouth away from London too, out of harm's way. But the lad was gone anyway. Racing, hunting, wenching no doubt. He smiled to himself. It was hardly the behaviour of one about to seize his father's crown.

He strolled to the canal in the park. He could feed the wild-fowl, he thought. Charles loved the country birds that clustered along the water's edge, as much at home in the heart of London as they would be in the innocent leafy fastnesses of the shires. Where Jemmie was. He fed the ducks in peace.

Later that morning he sailed downstream to Greenwich, for his five royal yachts – *Anne, Katherine, Charles, Jemmie* and *Henrietta* – were scheduled to race.

Charles sailed aboard *Katherine*; his brother, the Duke of York, captained *Anne*.

Charles, at *Katherine's* tiller, fixed his eyes on the two jibs forward. The brisk breeze kept them as full as a goodwife's belly, mused the king as he jockeyed for position with *Anne*. At first, they were side by side, but gradually *Katherine* pulled ahead. Charles was clearly the better skipper.

'On, on!' shouted the king. 'God for Charles and St George and Merry England!' The spray whipped his face. He exulted, his eyes flashing with delight at the wind-swept freedom of the sport. At last, as both yachts passed the Nore and entered the Channel, with the others still hull-down to their west, *Katherine*, in a sudden burst, left *Anne* far astern.

Charles could see James on the poop deck urging his seamen on. But *Katherine* was the clear winner, and Charles had stood himself in a hundred pounds, his wager with James.

So elated was the king that he scarcely noticed a small fishing smack across his bows a few cables' lengths ahead. Had he but known that, concealed in the small cabin was the Duke of Monmouth, outward bound from England for the Hook of Holland, he would have cracked on all sail and overhauled her. Instead Charles hove to and waited for *Anne* to catch him up.

'Well sailed, brother,' he called out in the teeth of the wind, 'but not quite well enough!'

The day ended in laughter and flagons of wine.

'Let me do it, Polly.' Bart pleaded with her passionately. 'There is no need to risk your life. The king does not demand it.' He had come to her chambers to try to dissuade her from plunging into dangers she did not comprehend, from doing anything that was foolhardy.

'Nor any need to risk yours, Bart.' Polly spoke firmly. She knew – she could not help but know – that only she was capable, perhaps with Whipt Ned's help, perhaps alone, of tracking the plotters through the ruins of the fire-devastated City. As a child, she had explored every one of those shadowy lanes and stifling alleys. Even with the landmarks burned to the ground, she was like a wild thing at home in its own jungle.

Bart was an outsider.

'Bart,' she said, 'you're very brave. But bravery has nothing to do with getting the evidence my lord of Clarendon requires.'

Bart put his arms around her. 'You make me feel so useless, Polly. Like an inept, unwanted child.'

Polly smiled into his eyes. 'You are, perhaps, not quite equipped to deal with mean people in mean streets. But unwanted? No. Never.'

'When must you go?'

'Kinnerton's man has instructions to prepare a coach for his lordship this night.'

'How do you know that?'

'Lord Clarendon is an old hand at espionage.'

'And tomorrow, at ebb tide? That is truly the moment chosen to abduct the king?'

'So it was decided at the Three Graces.'

She tried to slip from his embrace, but he clasped her waist more firmly. 'Polly, my love, – oh, how to say this, when you are balancing on the crater's edge of a volcano? – Polly, I beg you, try not to endanger yourself unduly.'

'Not unduly, Bart.' Her response was calm.

'Polly, Polly, listen to me. When all this is over, there is something I want to ask you.'

He trembled. She responded with a gentle vibrance coursing through her body.

'Ask me now.'

'No, Polly, I may not. For you are bounden in duty to the king. And I have no right to demand another promise from you.' He searched her eyes, worrying. 'Will Whipt Ned go with you?'

Polly nodded.

'He's a valorous man.'

'He's a sad thieving devil. But his heart is sound. Poor folk though my friends and neighbours may be, they are not the rats and vermin that the king's aristocracy take them for. Let but the call come to arms and they will fight as gallantly for His Majesty as Henry V's bowmen ever did at Agincourt. For are they not the same race, the same island people?'

'Indeed, Polly,' Bart said gravely. 'Then – God defend you.'

By now, so scrupulous was the watch kept by the beggars and rufflers of Bandyleg Lane on all strangers, that every move – no matter how discreet, no matter how well disguised – that Kinnerton and Galloping Jack made, was charted and reported to Whipt Ned. In Granny Fitch's kitchen, Ned passed the latest dispatches on to Polly.

'Pargiter has readied *Fancy Anne* for sea. She lies but on two hawsers, fore and aft. She is loading stores now.'

'Where is Galloping Jack?'

'We have lost his trail. But he has assembled a band of cut-throats. Jem Hoskin reported them moving west.'

'To Westminster?'

'Aye, I doubt not.' His forehead became corrugated with worried wrinkles. 'Poll, why should not the king send his soldiers? He could surround the ship –'

'I've told you, Ned, he won't. Only on proof –'

'What more proof is needed? Jack and Pargiter consort and plot with the Earl of Kinnerton! That is clear to see! A few hours on the rack – a twist or two of the thumbscrew – and they'll sing like nightingales.'

'That is not King Charles's way.'

She rose from the rough stool on which she had been sitting. 'Later, Ned, we shall board the ship. But first I am a-weary. I need sleep. I'll go to my gran's room. Meantime, await me.'

'Aye, Poll.'

Polly yawned deliberately and ostentatiously; then she entered the small back room where Granny Fitch slept. Ned watched her go. What a mort for a man to take a-begging on the king's highway! But he knew that this was only a dream. Much had happened to Polly in the past few days. She had already moved away from his world. Soon, he feared, they would say good-bye, and if he were ever to see her again, it would be no more than a tantalizing glimpse as she alighted from her coach with some great noble at her side. He felt melancholy. He rubbed his hands over the stubble on his chin. A rough face, and ugly. A poor man's face.

In Granny Fitch's narrow basement room, Polly quickly shed her feigned weariness. A small begrimed window pierced the heavy stone wall. She changed into her men's clothes, the king's breeches, tunic and hat, thrust the shutters back and slipped through the window into a ditch cluttered with the filth of ages. She leapt up to a tiny lane that ran behind the house. Evening surrounded her; the sound of voices was far away, as if on another planet. She walked briskly towards the waterside.

Fancy Anne's deck was covered with barrels and bales. Polly stood on the quay, her arms akimbo, watching as the crew manhandled them below. Near her, a gang of labourers unloaded still more cargo from a horse-drawn dray: flour, rum, gunpowder, cutlasses. She sauntered over to the foreman, and spoke in as gruff a voice as she could muster. 'Can you use a hand?' He glanced at her carelessly. 'Farthing a hundredweight, lad.' He studied her more closely. 'Slim-built, ben't you? Can you manage a man's load?'

She nodded, spat on her hands and, flexing her muscles, lifted a barrel of flour. She looked at him inquiringly. He grunted, 'You'll do.' Polly mounted a ramp to the deck and followed the others into the ship's hold.

Except for the chains and manacles fastened to the bulkheads, the slave deck was unrecognizable. Everywhere stood neatly-stacked containers of cargo. One had burst open and spilled forth bolts of bright printed cloth. Dozens of muskets were heaped on the deck, and kegs labelled 'Gunpowder' were ranged behind them towards the stern – coveted trade goods, these; for on the Guinea coasts, tribal clients were willing to give many slaves in exchange for arms and ammunition.

Let but a single spark, Polly reflected, penetrate the vessel's hold, and *Fancy Anne* would explode like a siege-bomb.

She set her barrel down among others in the provisions store, and then, taking advantage of the moment when the loaders started for the upper deck, slipped behind a barrier of boxes marked 'Pewter basons'. For an hour she waited, her thighs stiffening from the unaccustomed crouch. At length, the loading was completed. The last of the stevedores clattered down the ramp to shore, shouting and laughing.

And Polly was alone on the slave deck.

She came out cautiously from her hiding place. She heard Captain Pargiter call out overhead.

'All is prepared, my lord. The quarters below are arranged as you desired.'

'Then let us see them at once.' Polly bobbed quickly back behind her barricade, as Kinnerton and the captain descended the ladder to the slave deck. The two men peered about the dim hold.

'This way, my lord.'

Pargiter led Kinnerton aft, and for the first time Polly realized that a temporary bulkhead with a door had been erected across the deck, separating a small portion of the after end from the rest. The two men entered. Polly crept behind bales and barrels, inching silently towards them. She had had to deceive both Bart and Ned, but her plan had worked. She felt a *frisson*, part triumph and part fear.

Pargiter, just inside the temporary cabin, was showing it off, with malicious pride in his handiwork.

'We have, as you see, my lord, furnished it snugly. A pallet of straw, a table. And, should they be needed, manacles to restrain our guest's natural impetuosity.'

'He is a big man and strong,' said Kinnerton. 'Will this kennel hold him?'

Pargiter laughed.

'I warrant you, my lord. 'Tis not precisely Whitehall nor yet Hampton Court, but the gentleman has slept rough before. He will come to no harm during that portion of the journey which he is to share with us.' He shut the door, and the pair started back across the deck.

Now Polly, taking a deep unhappy breath, stepped into full view.

'Good evening, my lord,' she said in a clear firm tone.

Kinnerton swung towards her. Slowly a smile spread across his face.

'How delightful, Mistress Fitch! How very delightful to see you!'

'And how very surprising, my lord, to see you!'

'Nay, then, we are both surprised, are we not? I have been aware, mistress, of your interest in my movements. But I had hoped that it sprang merely from idle curiosity and that your gutter intelligence would have stopped you from venturing into an affair which is no concern of yours.'

'His Majesty's safety concerns everyone in his realm. As his loyal subject, my lord, I demand that you seize Captain Pargiter immediately, and hold him while I call the watch.'

Kinnerton began to chuckle.

'How very odd, my dear Polly. How very very odd. Here you stand, a prisoner, yet you give orders!'

'And am I then a prisoner?'

'Most assuredly. Pargiter, put this insolent, meddling woman in irons at once. It seems you will have a second passenger to the slave coast – or at least as far on the journey as His Majesty is bound.'

'Farther, my lord, if I may have your leave.' He stared at Polly. 'This is too rich a prize to consign to the bottom of the sea.'

Then he sprang towards her and clamped the manacles to her wrists. 'She will travel many leagues beyond her royal master. For there are black kings in Guinea who will pay well for such a one as she. If, that is,' he smirked questioningly, 'I may have your leave?'

'Do as you wish, captain,' said Kinnerton, mounting the ladder.

Pargiter chained Polly to the bulkhead, her hands and legs fettered to the solid oak, as though she were one of the hundreds of black slaves who had been transported across the world on this same deck. Then, without a word, he too left her.

She was a captive of the king's enemies. She had achieved her goal. Now, she prayed: let Bart and Ned have the wit to track her down and find her thus, and Clarendon will have evidence enough to hang every last conspirator who would plot to take the life of the king.

CHAPTER XI

THE CUNNING OF LADY CASTLEMAINE

Whipt Ned knew that he would be brusquely turned away if he tried to enter the Palace. Yet he must enter. He had waited patiently for Polly in the cellar outside Granny Fitch's little room. Hours had passed, and he began to worry. He knocked, knocked again and again, then stepped inside – and realized that she was gone. His duty was clear at once. He must find her.

She wouldn't simply have left without a word, he was sure of that. So Kinnerton and Galloping Jack must have discovered that she knew about their assassination plot, and abducted her to keep her quiet. In the hands of vicious men like those two, Polly's life would not be worth a penny.

But what could Ned do alone? He hesitated outside Whitehall, then squared his shoulders and walked up to an entrance. Londoners of all sorts were freely passing in and out, but the yeoman took one look at Ned and lowered his halberd.

'How now, fellow? We want no beggars here.'

Whipt Ned reddened with embarrassment. 'Truly, sir officer, I seek not to beg. But I must go inside. A life depends upon't.'

The yeoman laughed. 'To be sure, good Master Rags-and-Tatters! Whose life, if a humble soldier may ask?'

'The king's, sir.'

The yeoman burst into laughter and called to a colleague nearby. 'Come here, Matt. Here's a mad game to be sure! This rude fellow conceives himself to be the king's new champion. He seeks entry to Whitehall, and says if he gains it not, our royal master will lose his life!'

The second yeoman, over six feet tall, grey-bearded and gruff, stared down at Ned from his enormous height.

'So, you'd save the king, would you? Now, list to me, your noble lordship, you go back to your court of fools. Regale them with your bumpkin's pranks. But play me no nonsense games here.'

Ned jigged up and down in frustrated anger.

'Fools, is it? It's you that are the fools!'

Matt's face darkened with fury. 'Now I give you fair warning. Be gone and instantly, or we'll see what you have to say to a whipping.'

Ned stood firm. He had a duty! He wasn't the man to turn and run away. But he hadn't a clue as to what to do next. Then, as if Ned had sent for him, Bart Ravenscroft approached along King Street.

'There's one who'll vouch for me.'

Matt stared at the lean, elegant courtier. 'What? Master Ravenscroft? Why, he's a gentleman of the king's bedchamber. What business have you with him?'

Ned ignored him and limped hurriedly towards Bart.

'Master Ravenscroft, Master Ravenscroft –'

Bart stared at him puzzled, trying to recall him. Then he smiled his welcome. 'Why, it's Ned, is it not? Whipt Ned?' He gripped Ned's shoulder. 'Have you news of Polly?' Ned gulped and nodded. 'Come with me,' said Bart.

He swept him past the two astonished yeomen into the flowery quiet of the Privy Garden, and led Ned to a bench near the palace wall. 'Now, sit down, my good fellow, and tell me what has happened.'

The words poured out in a confused and worried gush.

'But why' Bart pondered, 'should she have left without you?'

Ned shook his head. 'Nay, master, that's more than I can say. She's a rare one, our Poll.'

'She would have had a very sound reason. Where think you she is now?'

'Aboard *Fancy Anne*, my lord.'

Bart shook his head. 'I'm no lord, Ned, only Bart Ravenscroft. Esquire, if you will – but no more. When do you say the ship weighs anchor?'

'Tonight, at eleven of the clock, on the ebb tide.'

Bart rose abruptly from the bench. 'Come with me. This time the king cannot choose but listen. But first we must have a council of war. And there are, indeed, but a scant few hours in which to accomplish all.'

On the slave deck of *Fancy Anne*, Polly Fitch, spreadeagled against the bulkhead, felt a growing weariness. If only she could sit down, lie down. Her muscles ached with strain. She let her arms and body sag, but as the chains took her full weight, white-hot pain stabbed through her legs and arms. The manacles bit deep into her wrists. She straightened up again.

Had she been a fool? Would Whipt Ned realize what had happened? Hers had been a desperate measure, to offer up her life thus, to save the king's; and to rely for the success of her stratagem on Ned's being astute enough to reach the right conclusion, and to take the right steps.

If help came at all, would it come too late? She had no way of knowing how many hours had already dragged by; in the twilight of the stifling, stinking slave deck, she could not hope to measure the passage of time, unless by the steady increase of pain within her body.

She listened despairingly for the footsteps of rescuers trampling on the deck above, for the clash of steel. But only the unfamiliar cries of the sailors readying the vessel for sea came to her through the half-closed hatches. Polly's shoulders drooped with weariness. Again that blinding dagger thrust through her muscles. 'Dear Jesu,' she prayed, 'give Whipt Ned the loan of a good brain, only for a little while – only for long enough to save King Charles's life! And mine, sweet Jesu, and mine too!'

In Lord Clarendon's book-lined room, Whipt Ned sat awkwardly on the same high-backed chair that Polly had sat in when she, Bart and Lady Castlemaine had come to seek the sage old courtier's counsel. The king's mistress and his Gentleman of the Bedchamber were both here again. In such company, Ned was tongue-tied with embarrassment, yet desperately eager to say what he had come to say.

Clarendon listened judiciously to his halting narrative. The lawyer's brow wrinkled, the long brown forefingers made their usual miniature steeple upon the table. Then, tugging gently at his wispy beard, Clarendon questioned Ned as though he were a witness in a courtroom.

'When she told you she wished to rest, did she look extremely exhausted?'

'No, my lord.'

'And you sat just outside the room into which she had retired?'

'Granny Fitch's room, yes, my lord.'

'How far from the door were you seated?'

'I was nearer to it than I am now to you.'

'If Mistress Fitch had made any sound – had there been any sort of struggle – would you have heard it?'

'I would, my lord.'

'If one of these men had come to abduct her, what think you, Ned? Would she have gone quietly?'

'No, my lord. She would have fought like a catamount, all teeth and claws.'

'I'll vouch for that!' Lady Castlemaine smiled ironically.

'Could she have been lured away – by some false promise or hope of gain?'

Ned looked puzzled. 'My lord?'

Bart broke in. 'I think not, Lord Clarendon. Polly is neither a fool nor a traitor.'

'Then,' Clarendon concluded, 'she went of her own free will.'

'To the slave ship, I have no doubt, my lord,' Bart interposed. 'But what I cannot riddle is why she should have gone alone. She most assuredly would have known that, had she permitted Ned to go along, she would have had a far better chance to prove what she wanted to prove, and to get away safely. But alone, even though she is strong and agile, she must inevitably have been caught. She must have known that, too.'

'You mean, then,' Clarendon asked, 'that she quite deliberately set out to be caught? That she wanted to be trapped? Why on earth should that be so?'

'To understand such a topsy-turvy motivation, my lord,' Barbara Castlemaine said, 'you must examine the ways of women. Why, indeed! You have no one to ask but yourself. It was you who sent her on this mission. Proof, you demanded! Irrefutable evidence, you insisted – if the king were to be convinced. Well, what stronger evidence than to force Kinnerton, to trick him and his minions into capturing her?

'She took a daring risk, gentlemen – in some circumstances, women do. She staked her life against odds – the odds that we must all divine what she had done, and come to her aid in time. Thus, the murdering rogues would be apprehended in the very commission of a crime – lesser, of course, than encompassing the death of the king, but a part of the very plot, great enough to show them for what they are.'

Clarendon looked at her admiringly. 'If it were not for your sex, my lady, I should swear you'd been reared a Jesuit!'

Barbara slightly inclined her beautiful head, in acknowledgement of his grudging compliment. 'Are you thus unriddled now, Master Ravenscroft?'

'Yes,' said Bart as he rose. 'I am off to seek audience of the king.'

'Not yet,' Barbara raised her white, heavily-ringed hand. 'Before that, we must be certain that all is, indeed, as I said.' She smiled her radiant smile. 'It was only a woman's speculation, after all. But I must now find out whether or no I have hazarded correctly.'

'How will you do that?' Clarendon asked.

'I have some influence with the Earl of Kinnerton, my lord. He thinks himself the cleverest man at court. That shall be my weapon against him. For there is none so stupid, as I am sure your lordship knows, as a vainly self-confident and exceedingly clever man.'

Said Clarendon, 'I leave it to you, then, to choose your time.' He looked over his shoulder, at an ornate clock on the mantel. 'But it had best be soon.'

Even so, after Ned and Ravenscroft had left the room, Barbara lingered.

'My lord of Clarendon.' Her tone was unwontedly hesitant. 'Yes, madame?'

'You are writing a history of these stormy times, I believe?'

'Indeed, madame.'

'And will you include this – episode?'

'I have not yet given it much thought.'

'Might I beg you to suppress the matter?'

Lord Clarendon raised his eyebrows. 'Would it be impertinent, seeming to pry, to inquire into the reason?'

Barbara bit her full lower lip.

'I had rather you did not.'

'I could the more readily accede to your wish, countess, if I understood the reason for it.'

His words were gently spoken, but his tone suggested a greater firmness than the syllables conveyed.

'Lord Clarendon, we are, are we not, friends?'

'No, madame.' He smiled politely. 'Not friends, no.'

'You will record me, in your history, as you see me, no doubt. The king's mistress, desirous, avaricious, acquisitive, sometimes spiteful – a dangerous enemy?'

'This day's tender understanding of another woman's plight, madame,' Clarendon smiled wryly; 'will unquestionably soften any portrait I might paint.'

She shook her head. 'Suppress this incident, my dear lord. I hate her! Detest her for her self-seeking arrogance. I do what I do only for the love of Charles.'

'I see. You do not wish credit where none is due you?'

Lady Castlemaine smiled. 'So tactful a courtier. Even to the end?'

'Even to the end, my lady.'

'Then I pray you, when you come to write, do not blacken the character of your old enemy with one good deed.'

Clarendon's eyes betrayed just a trace of a twinkle.

'As your ladyship wishes.'

Gracefully she courtseyed. Stiffly the old man bowed. And silently Lady Castlemaine withdrew.

Left alone, Clarendon looked bemusedly at the stacks of manuscript pages he had covered in his neat hand over the years. Should a historian tell the truth? His sound conservative instincts told him that the answer was yes. But he had given Barbara Castlemaine his word. And so she must be presented to future ages as a wicked, scheming bitch. Why did she wish it so?

He smiled to himself: some women were enamoured of wickedness, he supposed. Their instincts were sound. For what was a woman's driving force? To gain the attention of men. And virtue had few powers of attraction. One might well admire Mary of Nazareth, but he'd never heard of any man who wished to sleep with her. While the unabashedly scheming and evil Messalina – well, that was another matter entirely.

If Satan had been a woman, he reflected, one would scarce have been able to insinuate a sedan chair through the crowds battering to force their way in at the door.

Then another thought struck him. Men, it came to him in a flash, were far less devious than women. If he were to conceal Barbara's one good deed, then he was trapped, was he not, into suppressing the far greater heroism of Polly Fitch? He chuckled: Oh, the cunning of Lady Castlemaine!

Well, what did history matter after all? He had performed one more service for his king. Perhaps the last. He walked to the mounted globe and spun it until France – fair smiling France – lay before him. A young man's country. Still, it would see him through. Yes, when Charles dismissed him, he would die in France.

The Earl of Kinnerton walked out upon the roof of Whitehall. Below, the river ran, shining, smooth, glinting like metal in the misty afternoon light. Soon the sun would set, the tide would turn, and then, and then . . . His eyes swung downstream to where, beyond the Thames's great sweeping curve, lay the Guinea-bound ship, *Fancy Anne*. Already Galloping Jack's men stood at the ready in a house in St James's, tensed and eager for their assault upon the king. Young Jemmie, Duke of Monmouth, awaited his signal in the Hague.

Kinnerton allowed his mind to turn to the wench, Polly, fettered on the slave deck. What a waste! What a fool he had been not to have supped from that sumptuous platter that had delivered itself up to him!

Ah, well, he could take what women he wanted, once stupid

Jemmie was on the throne. For all the bastard might call himself king, he himself would be the one who pulled the strings. He would charm the foolish lad – cajole him – and not try to argue or to reason, as the doting old Clarendon did with Charles.

What fragile mortals kings were! So easily manoeuvred – given that the manoeuverer was endowed with craft, wit and a flatterer's tongue.

He heard a footstep behind him. A soft feminine arm slipped through his.

'Brooding, my lord of Kinnerton? Or perhaps composing another of your delightfully wicked verses?' The sparkling eyes of Barbara Castlemaine looked invitingly up into his own.

'I was contemplating the beauty of the scene,' Kinnerton replied. 'But since your coming, my lady, 'tis rivalled and indeed outshone.'

Lady Castlemaine cast down her eyes. She sighed. 'Alas, I am the she who is rivalled and outshone. The moon blotted by Venus.'

'You?' Kinnerton and Barbara walked slowly across the roof, arm in arm. 'May I exercise my art in this matter?'

'Pray do.'

He closed his eyes. His lips moved but without sound. His free hand seemed to mark some unheard rhythm. Then he spoke.

> ' "I ruled the skies," fair Diane said,
> But now my rule's in vain.
> Another's come to quench my light.
> Her name? Why, Castlemaine!'

'How gracefully you comfort a poor rejected lady!' Barbara replied. 'Yet though I outsilver Diana, the moon goddess, there is one in this court who outsilvers me.' Again she sighed. 'Heigh-ho, my dear lord. I shall retire to the country and grow strawberries.'

He paused. Such a beautiful mouth!

'Then must you force nature to match the ruby of your lips.'

He lowered his head, and kissed, where Charles so often

kissed. Lady Castlemaine turned her head aside. A tear shone
on her long lashes.

'Tears, Lady Barbara? Are my kisses so unwelcome?'

'Unwelcome? Never, Lord Kinnerton. But I could promise
greater rewards than kisses to the man who would –'

'Would what?'

'I shame to say it. Would rid me of that low-born vixen,
Polly Fitch. I wish this not for myself alone. She degrades the
court, the king, all here in Whitehall!'

Kinnerton eyed her again, measuring her contours calculatingly. An anticipatory glow suffused him. To embrace the
king's whore after displacing the king himself, there would be
triumph indeed!

'Then hark, Barbara. I shall claim that reward.'

'How? Will you remove her from Westminster?'

'I have already done so.'

'But she will return.'

'She can never return.'

'Is she – dead?'

'Not yet. But her passport to death is already written.'

'You would not commit murder?'

'No need. Polly shall live, but a living death. Far from here,
until her beauty withers beneath the African sun and her body,
sucked dry of all delight, is cast aside by some barbarian black
lord on the Guinea coast.'

Barbara could scarcely hide the tremor that shook her voice.
'You would send her to Africa?'

'She is already aboard the vessel, *Fancy Anne*. She sails on
the ebb tide.'

'This, my lord,' said Barbara in a voice as calculatingly cold
as an iceberg, 'is splendid news. But why have you chosen to do
it? How has the minx offended you?'

'As she has you, my lady. She o'erstepped the bounds. She
came between me and my sovereign king.'

Barbara threw her arms around him.

'What good fortune, then. Our ends are one and the same.'

'And I may trust you to deliver to me my – reward?'

'Yes.'

137

'Barbara, when? When may I claim what is my due?'

'Your due, my dear Lord Kinnerton,' she looked deeply into his eyes, 'your due will be delivered to you after the tide has turned.' He tried once more to kiss her, but she turned aside.

'No more now, sweet sir. Rewards, like wine, are all the better for the keeping.'

She hastened down to the gardens below. Kinnerton felt a surge of delight. The chancellor to the new King Jemmie! And to be the lover of the most desired woman in all the land! No heights were beyond him now. 'Ah,' he murmured aloud, 'to have been given brains – and then to have the brains to use them!'

In his privy chamber, Charles surveyed Barbara with amused puzzlement. Bart stood beside her, shifting impatiently from foot to foot. No matter what the urgency, there was no way the young man could cut short the courtly badinage.

'If I did not know you so well, my dear one, I would think that you had turned charitable and Christian. To forgive poor Polly after she ruined your gown and marinated, as the French cooks say, your beautiful coif in my best claret!'

'I am as good a Christian as Your Majesty may hope to see in this wicked world. Is forgiveness to be the province of men alone, and magnanimity confined to kings?'

Charles laughed. 'Never, Barbara. But I suspect that your open-heartedness is that of a money lender. You give, only to gain a greater return.'

'If you think that of me, my liege, I will –' she restrained a bubble of mirth as she thought of Kinnerton '– retire to the country and grow strawberries!'

'And I shall retire with you and milk the cows for cream. But come, whatever your motive, I am now convinced that you are right, both you and Bart. The time for kingly hesitation has passed.' He rose to his feet abruptly. 'I thank you, Barbara. You may withdraw. Ravenscroft and I have men's work on our hands.'

Lady Castlemaine curtseyed and left the room, with a

conspiratorial glance over her shoulder at Charles. But he was already deeply involved with Bart. His face was grave.

'Good sir, good friend that you are, I can speak my mind to you openly.' He gazed out the window, up into the softly-lit sky. Then he turned back, choosing his words one by one, like a good housewife picking the best cherries from a basket.

'This odious matter involves my son. By happenstance, I truly believe, and not of his own volition. Still, I would not have it bruited about the court. And yet, Mistress Polly must be rescued.'

He shouted, 'Chiffinch.'

The valet entered soundlessly.

'My lord?'

'Master Ravenscroft and I go to the City this evening. Have a light four-oared craft, with no royal markings of any sort, waiting at the privy steps just after sunset.'

'Very good, sire.'

The king turned a stern face upon him. 'This is no frivolous tryst, no lightsome dalliance, but an affair of state. I go in secret, with no ceremony.'

'Yes, my lord.'

'And mark you, Will, not a word to any soul in this palace – or on this earth!

Chiffinch bowed.

'Then see to it straightaway.'

The valet backed out. Charles turned to Bart.

'Are you a swordsman?'

'My master was Niccolo of Florence.'

Charles gripped him approvingly by the shoulder. 'The best teacher of the art, whether with poignard or rapier, south of the Alps.'

'He taught me to fight with both, sire. Sword and dagger at the same time.'

'Would that we each had three hands, Bart. Or even six. They'll be well-stocked with strong-armed rogues aboard *Fancy Anne*.'

'You would risk your own life, sire? But you must not! Polly has woven this scheme to keep you from danger, not to thrust you in its midst! I can choose good sturdy men from among your guard. And brave. We'll clean out that vessel as you scoop honey from a hive.'

Charles shook his head, then smiled.

'I haven't drawn sword since the battle of Worcester, Bart. I grow rusty in my old age. The exercise will do me good.' He went on seriously, 'Nay, Bart. The cause is my own life, is it not? And whose life, in such a cause, has the king a better right to jeopardize? We'll have your Polly out of danger, never fear.'

Bart flushed.

'*My* Polly?'

'Do you not consider her so? Come, Bart, your king has his moments of folly. But he is not quite a fool.'

On the slave deck, Polly's muscles sagged. The manacles bit cruelly. A film like cobweb drifted across her eyes. She fought against the faintness that was overwhelming her.

Fancy Anne was silent, save for the creaking of timbers and the ripple of water, dimly heard, as the incoming tide lapped against the ship's sturdy hull.

CHAPTER XII

EBB TIDE

In Will Chiffinch's little room above the privy steps, the king and Bart bent over a set of tide tables. 'The tide presses upstream, sire, until five and twenty minutes past nine this evening. By ten o'clock, the ebb begins. *Fancy Anne* is due to cast off at eleven. She lies just below London Bridge.'

'That means,' the king pondered, 'that if we are to return in time to catch these rogues in Whitehall in the act of abstracting our royal person, we have our evening's work cut out. Look you, Bart, we must pull downstream against the tide to rescue Polly, then upstream, once more against the tide.

He paused. 'We cannot do it. Not fighting the stream both ways! If we arrive back here too late, the rogues, finding no king, will simply melt away like mist. And they must be taken in the act. Otherwise I'm doomed to sit in my palace like an earthed fox, with no idea when the hunters may return.'

'True, sire. Yet it must be done.'

Charles pushed the tide tables aside, and strode to the door. 'Wait here for me an instant, Bart. Or better, get you down the stairs to our boat and be ready to cast off as soon as I step aboard.' He hurried out of the room.

Bart descended a narrow passage and came out on the tiny pier the king used for water journeys. A small skiff lay at the end of the jetty, straining upstream against its moorings as the tidal surge tugged painfully. Bart loosened the lines until the vessel was held by only a single rope. Then he arranged a slip knot: one pull would set the craft loose. Finally he stepped aboard and took the bow oars. The free end of the slip knot lay ready to his hand.

His eye was fixed on the gate at the jetty's landward end. It swung open. Bart's hand tightened on the rope. But it was not Charles. Instead he saw small bustling Lord Clarendon.

'Where is the king?' the old earl demanded.

'Within, my lord. I wait upon him now.'

'Then listen,' Clarendon bent down towards Bart. 'I am informed that strangers have made their way into Whitehall. Tall strapping men, all wearing outlandish garments. They are drifting in twos and threes along the galleries. A yeoman challenged one, who brushed him aside and told him that he had been summoned to perform in a royal masque.'

'There is no masque tonight,' Bart said, bewildered.

'I know that. These men are not what they seem, Bart, nor what they proclaim themselves to be.'

'Where are they?'

Clarendon shook his head. 'Scattered. I know not where. I set some of my fellows to track them down, but they returned empty-handed. They have vanished in this royal wilderness of Whitehall. There's mischief in it, my boy.'

'How did you know I was here?' Bart asked suddenly. 'The king did not tell you?'

'No, lad. He did not, indeed. But I have a head on my shoulders still, and can reason beyond the present as well as most men. You are to row the king downstream, are you not? To free Mistress Polly?'

Bart nodded.

'And tonight the vessel sails. Intending to bear the king's person as its golden cargo. Does the plot not run so? Dead or alive, will he or nill he, King Charles is to be carried off.'

'Yes.'

'Then these false masquers are the villains who mean to do it. I shall –'

'No, my lord. Do not summon the guard, I pray you – if that is what you were about to say. The king wants no whisper of this matter to be heard.'

'Because of Monmouth's involvement?'

'Aye, my lord.'

'And yet, the masquers must be laid by the heels. How can that be done in secret? What say you?'

Bart's brain was working furiously. An idea burst upon him. 'My lord of Clarendon, Whipt Ned's your man. Send to

Ned – he lives near Granny Fitch's in Bandyleg Lane. No, stay. Do not send. Go yourself. He has a band of sturdy beggars at his whistle. Return with them, and plant me a guard hidden about the king's quarters. A half dozen will do, for I shall be there too. I shall return, once we have freed Polly.'

'Setting rogues to catch rogues.' Clarendon chuckled. 'A shrewd scheme!'

'Then make haste.' Bart's voice was urgent. 'And God go with you to Bandyleg Lane, my lord!'

Clarendon bustled back into the palace. 'I was wrong,' he muttered to himself with pleasure, as he made his way towards King Street. 'I have not done my last service for Charles Stuart, after all.' He stepped into a hackney coach. 'Bandyleg Lane, my man – and double fare if you make it in half an hour.'

A crack of the whip, and the coach rumbled off over the cobbles.

At the privy steps, Charles appeared, wrapped in a boat cloak, his plumed hat pulled down over his eyes. He stepped in and took the stern oars laughing. 'A primitive disguise Bart, but effective. Would you believe it? I passed Sam Pepys, but a moment ago, and he, who prides himself on seeing all and knowing all, did not recognize me. 'Tis indeed the purple and fine linen that make the king.'

Bart silently swung the bow downstream. So powerful was the tide that the tiny craft almost turned full circle to face upstream again. But Charles gave a mighty pull, the skiff straightened and her bow dipped into the strongly-running wavelets.

A sharp wind blew from the east, adding to the difficulty of making headway. Charles grunted. 'An ill wind that bloweth no man to good, as John Heywood said in his proverbs.'

'Not so, sire,' Bart contradicted. 'For this wind must needs delay *Fancy Anne,* as well. Where is the seaman who can sail into the wind's eye in so narrow a river as Thames?'

They pulled on in silence. 'True,' Charles finally replied. 'If the Lord must send his winds against us, 'tis only just he should send them likewise against our enemies.'

Never easing, breathing hard, without a word, they worked their way past the palaces that lined the Strand – Northumberland House, the rebuilt palace of Savoy, noble Somerset House. Now they were abreast of the smooth green lawns of the Temple, and a straight reach of the river lay before them, crowded with wherries, barges and skiffs.

A gloriously caparisoned galley shot out from an inlet on the south bank and cut across their bows. Eight richly uniformed rivermen plied their oars in perfect unison. Charles and Bart backed water, but the tide swept them on and the two boats almost collided. The hoarse voice of the galley's skipper reached them across the few yards that lay between.

'Make way, you two, for the king's barge. Way, I say, or I'll swamp you!'

Bart lifted his oars in acquiescence. The royal barge glided by, looming over them.

'Od's fish,' Charles remarked mildly, 'to be given the rough side of his tongue by my own bargemaster. It passes belief, Bart!'

Now, rising ahead of them, an ominous barrier with its twenty arches, was London Bridge. The water grew increasingly turbulent: each arch formed a sort of small mill-race through which the incoming tide roared, compressed by the piers to either side.

'Bart,' the king called out against the wind, 'we must steer for the centre opening. 'Tis by far the broadest and least likely to send us to the bottom. I've done this before. 'Tis a rare trial of a man's skill with the oars.'

The water lashed into a surging, angry foam as the centre channel pushed against them, trying to force them back.

'We'll need all our strength now,' the king said, 'or we'll be food for the fishes. Pull Bart, pull!'

Their bow at last pointed towards the opening. The skiff twisted and whirled. Flashes of light bounced and fragmented in the bubbling water, reflections from the windows of shops and houses on the old span. As they fought their way into the arch, Bart glanced upward and caught a glimpse of a woman silhouetted between two candle flames at a window.

The boat lurched against one stanchion, ricocheted and leapt forward into total darkness. London Bridge hung directly above their heads. Over the river's roar, they could hear the rhythmic clatter of horses' hooves on the bridge's wooden roadway. They strained at their oars, grappling with the tide as if it were a wild animal. One moment they vanquished, the next they were hurled back. Little by little they gained with anguishing, frightening slowness.

Then, with a jolt, they were through, the violence of the current eased. They slipped out into the reach called the Pool of London.

In the eerie quiet, the king spoke. 'Well done, Bart. Do you know that Sam Pepys is so terrified to do what we have just done that he deserts his craft upstream of the bridge, walks around on dry land and rejoins the vessel only after the bridge is safely behind him. And Mr Pepys, God save us, is the secretary to my navy!'

The king's jollity faded. His eyes swept the north bank. 'God save us indeed,' he muttered half to himself. 'Here is a sight to freeze the blood.'

It was. Downstream from the bridge, the worst havoc left by the Great Fire was cruelly apparent. Houses, mansions, wharves, churches, all blackened, destroyed. Charles stared at the ruins of a huge waterside fortress. Its walls had cracked in the enormous heat, and now lay in sooty mountains of masonry. Two turrets alone remained intact rearing black against the purple-blue sky.

'Baynard's Castle' said the king. 'I supped there with the Earl of Sandwich in the year of my return from exile.'

He rested on his oars and stared downstream. The vast bulk of the Tower of London stood unscathed. A little to its west was a wharf. A lone vessel lay alongside, her prow facing downstream. The sails were loosened from the yards but not yet unfurled. Lanterns hung from the mast-heads, and two more shone at the corners of the sterncastle, their rays making little pirouettes as they glanced off the swirling water.

'Softly now, Bart,' said the king. 'I think this is our goal. Three masts, square-rigged on the fore and main, but lateen on

145

the mizzen. Row ahead a little but gently and thence to the larboard.'

In the shadows of night, the tiny skiff edged towards the vessel.

'She lies low in the water,' Charles commented, 'so she's already fully laden. And look you, Bart, her sails are unclewed.'

They edged the skiff to the ship's side, and then, taking care not to bump against her hull, paddled rather than rowed towards the stern. Charles shipped his oars and caught a rope that trailed from the poop. Light flowed from the captain's cabin. They could hear a murmur of voices. Someone laughed. There was a clink of tankards.

'Can you make out her name?' the king asked. As Charles held on to the rope, Bart rose precariously in the rocking skiff to decipher the faded letters that ran athwart the stern.

'*Fancy Anne*, sire,' he whispered.

Heavy footsteps echoed on the poop. A head and shoulders appeared, outlined against the starlight, leaning over the railing just above them. They held their breaths. The man looked down. But the pair were sheltered in the deep shadow of the cabin's overhang.

Unexpectedly, the skiff bobbed, thrusting against the heavy shaft of the rudder. Wood rubbed against wood with a soft creak. The lookout again glanced down, but he saw nothing. Then he disappeared, but they could still hear his feet, pacing on the poop.

'All quiet,' he called out. 'Pass the word.' A pause, then a second more distant voice repeated the cry. 'All quiet.' And from other parts of the main deck the call was heard again and again.

Bart wiped his forehead, surprised to find that he had been sweating. 'They keep good watch, sire,' he whispered.

'But not quite good enough.' Charles's face, half-hidden in the murky darkness, was set. 'Have you ever shed blood, Bart?' His voice was so quiet as to be almost inaudible.

'No, sire.'

'You will do so tonight.'

The footsteps on the poop receded.

'My lord?'

'Yes?'

'How shall we avoid the watch?'

'Either we fight our way,' said the king, 'or a miracle intervenes.'

'If we must fight, only to get aboard, then the alarm is raised throughout the vessel. God knows what they will have done to Polly before we can hope to find her.'

'Miracles,' Charles said reassuringly, 'sometimes occur exactly when they are needed most. Or what seem to be miracles. Although, in my belief, the seemingly miraculous often conceals the agency of a human being.'

The water around the skiff was still, dark, almost viscous, like oil. The river seemed bewitched, strangely tranquil.

'I think, sire,' said Bart, 'that the incoming tide is done. We hang now upon the flood.'

Hooves in the distance clattered towards the waterfront – at first the sound of one horse, then of several, multiplying and overlaying each other, the jingle of harness and the snort of the beasts.

On the deck, there was a flurry of running feet.

'Who goes there below?' a rough voice shouted from the ship. The watch rushed to the bulwarks on the landward side.

'The miracle has come, Bart,' said the king. 'Quick! To the starboard and over the gunwales.'

In an instant they had clambered up. The deck lay almost empty beneath the cold light of the lanterns. The crew stood clustered along the opposite railing, looking down at the wharf.

'Come,' Charles whispered. A hatch gaped open. With their hands on their sword hilts, they crept softly towards it.

Lord Clarendon, amused, surprised and delighted, jounced back in his coach towards Whitehall, from his parley with Whipt Ned. He and his coachmen had become almost hopelessly lost in their search for him; but they had, at last, found Granny Fitch's kitchen – and in it, Ned. 'How little,' Clarendon thought, 'I know of London now. Such an antiquity I've become.' Yet, why should an aging statesman be familiar with the lanes and alleys of the post-Restoration, post-fire City of London? The thought restored his self-esteem.

Whipt Ned, meantime, at home in the maze, had set out recruiting at once. And now, by numerous secret routes, the beggars of Bandyleg Lane were swiftly moving westward to the palace.

Well, Clarendon reflected, I have done what I could. I am accustomed to more conventional means of dealing with sedition. But young Bart Ravenscroft may well be right. *Autres temps, autres moeurs,* he mused, remembering his exiled years in France – years long gone, when Charles still respected him as the most senior and most sapient of his advisers. Other times, other ways. His coach clattered on through Fleet Street towards the Strand.

The great hall of the palace, not long since fitted out by the play-loving king as a theatre, was lit by a few candles. Upon the stage clustered a bizarre gathering of men in the guise of wild beasts. A yeoman of the guard shouldered his way in. 'Who be you all, my masters?'

Kinnerton, suave in his usual elegant court clothes, stepped forward from the midst of the shaggy two-legged creatures.

'You wished to ask me something?' The yeoman bowed, abashed. 'My Lord of Kinnerton, I was unaware of your presence.'

Kinnerton smiled. 'Not at all, captain. You but do your duty. These people are players – masquers – in the entertainment that is toward, for His Majesty's pleasure.'

'Your pardon, my lord.' The yeoman backed out, pausing at the door to stammer, 'I – I was not informed.' Outside a small quiet man in a snuff-coloured jerkin eyed him sharply. 'Well, captain?'

'You may tell his lordship of Clarendon,' returned the soldier irritably, 'that all is in order. They are players, vouched for by the Earl of Kinnerton.'

Clarendon's spy raised his eyebrows. 'Of what sort are they?'

'Nay, I understand not these matters. They wore the heads of animals – lions, jackasses, catamounts. 'Tis some fable of the beasts, no doubt. Some drollery the earl has fabricated.'

'Kinnerton, eh?' The man in the snuff-coloured clothes moved softly away.

In the great hall, Kinnerton was rehearsing his troupe. 'Now roar me a good roar, lion!'

The tall fellow with the tawny lion's head upon his shoulders emitted a terrific bellow.

'Now, jackass, bray! Good!' Kinnerton looked about at the masquers. 'Catamount, a yowl to raise the dead!' A horrifying screech came from the man dressed as a mountain cat. He leaped three feet into the air, and Kinnerton nodded. 'Good, excellent! Now, Galloping Jack and all of you, spread out through the palace. Roar! Bray!

'Have no fear of attracting attention. In these chambers foolish capers are as much at home as Ave Marias in a cathedral.' The beasts loped towards the door.

'Stay a moment,' Kinnerton added. 'Remember, with each howl and bray and roar, every man must move always towards the place of rendezvous. And forget not, you are but masquers. Keep your blades concealed until they are called for.'

Mopping and mowing, the rogues did as they were bid. Ladies of the court pretended fright as they approached, but giggled when the lion shook his long, tangled mane, the catamount pawed lewdly at their breasts and the jackass brayed obscenities in their ears. In the court of good King Charles, the normal might indeed be noted. But, as Kinnerton knew so well, all that was outlandish had ready acceptance. It was the age of the eccentric, and Charles's royal court was the very breeding ground of fantasy.

Weird shadows played against the walls as the masquers skipped, pranced, cavorted. Torchlight lit the pagan heads of the unreal animals dancing through the doorways and up the narrow stairs, moving closer and ever closer to the privy apartments of the king.

At one point a small guard passed, escorting a trio of Queen Catherine's Portuguese nuns, who shrank among their protectors. The invaders drew back with mocking politeness to the walls, dropping to their knees and mimicking the sign of the cross. The nuns hurried on. And the beasts pursued their shadowy gyrations with soft-footed obscenity.

The gentle black-robed women crossed themselves. 'Mary Mother of Jesu, preserve us this night!'

Polly hung unconscious in her chains. As the king stood guard with bared sword at the foot of the ladder leading to the slave quarters, Bart withdrew the metal bolts from the manacles that pinioned her wrists and ankles. She moaned softly as he lowered her to the deck. Taking a dipper of water from an open barrel, he bathed her face, gently dabbing at the closed eyelids, at the pale lips. Gradually, pink flushed back into her cheeks. She sat up rubbing her wrists and blinking in the light of two lanterns that swung from the planking above. Her eyes focussed on Bart.

'Polly,' he whispered urgently, 'Polly, my love!'

'Bart!' Her arms went around his neck. 'How do you come here?'

He helped her to her feet. 'Ned. He feared for you. But you will hear all later. Now we must get you out of this stinking place.'

She stood swaying slightly, still clinging to Bart for support; then her eyes turned towards Charles – grim, motionless, poised to fight. Her mouth fell open, 'Your Majesty!'

Charles put his finger to his lips, 'Hush, Poll.'

Shakily, she made as if to curtsey.

He smiled. 'No need for that.'

Heavy footsteps trampled overhead, approaching the open hatch. The king reached up and unhooked one of the lanterns. 'Take the other, Bart.'

Timbers creaked just above them. Charles motioned Polly and Bart into the recess behind the ladder. He ducked in beside them. 'Keep well back, Poll,' Bart whispered. But Polly shook her head, and produced from beneath her jerkin the tiny dagger that he had given her in his chamber. 'I fight beside you, Bart.'

Pargiter came slowly down the ladder, holding a lantern and

peering about cautiously. He swung the light towards the bulkhead where Polly had been tethered. Only empty manacles! Baffled, he stepped down to the deck and saw at once the three half-shadowed faces behind the ladder's rungs. He roared, 'George, Ben, quick!' He drew his sword and holding his lantern high above his head, advanced. His eyes widened as he recognized Charles.

'So, Your Majesty, you have decided to save us the trouble of escorting you to *Fancy Anne*. You come of your own will. How good of you.'

Charles walked forward, his sword gleaming, his own light held so that its glimmer fell on Pargiter's grinning face.

'Are you the captain of this vessel?'

'I am.'

'Then I call upon you, as your king, to surrender it to my keeping at once, and to place your men under my command. You will have a fair trial and may cite whatever evidence you wish in your own defence.'

Pargiter laughed hoarsely but nervously.

'I'm afraid the boot's on the other leg, sire.' Three sailors, all armed, clattered down from the main deck. Pargiter turned to them. 'Behold, a bird that seeks its own cage.'

One of them whispered, almost in awe, 'The king!'

'Surrender to me instantly,' Charles thundered in a voice that rang with majesty. 'On your knees, all of you.'

The sailors hesitated. Their eyes swung, bewildered, from Charles's stern face to that of their captain.

'Fall on,' cried Pargiter. 'It's four of us to two of them.'

'Three!' Polly sprang forward, her body crouched. Bart's poignard glinted in her hand.

Pargiter rushed at the king. With a sliding clash their two sword blades met. The sailors swung on Bart and Polly.

Pargiter, rough and muscular though he was, was no match for Charles. It took the king, who had been trained by the finest masters in Europe, scarcely a moment to realize that the skipper was a clumsy swordsman. With a swift alternation of feints and lunges, Charles drove Pargiter back across the deck; the tip of his blade flickered within inches of the seaman's breast-bone. Then, Pargiter, his lantern held aloft, backed towards the gunpowder barrels that were massed at the after end of the deck. He stumbled, dropped his guard. The king swiftly and efficiently passed his blade through his chest.

Pargiter fell backwards against the kegs, his sword flying through the air in a glittering arc, his lantern soaring out of his hand to tumble, like a sparkling Catherine Wheel to the deck.

Charles looked down at his fallen foe. The body shuddered, twisted, then lay still.

The king now turned to join the second scuffle. Bart and Polly, forced into the narrowing bows, were barely managing to hold their own. The three seamen, their cutlasses flailing crudely like scythes, pressed them further and further back.

'Turn, you dogs,' Charles shouted. Two of the men swung about. Bart engaged the third, driving him towards the centre of the deck. There was an undisciplined mêlée as the five fought together, their blades clashing, Bart and the king illuminating the battle with the lanterns in their hands.

A cutlass whistled down. Bart cried out and sank to his knees. The blade had taken him in the arm. The sailor who had wielded it leaned over, his bloody cutlass raised above Bart's throat.

A fierce primitive scream stopped him in mid-thrust. Polly, her face contorted by anger and hatred, had leaped forward. Charles saw her hand lift, saw the poignard flash. She caught the man squarely between his shoulders.

'Up to the main deck, Poll, quickly, while I hold them off,' the king called. She hesitated, reluctant to leave the wounded Bart. 'Go, girl, go!' Charles's voice was urgent. 'I'll see to him.' Polly scaled the ladder while the king engaged both his adversaries at the same time. It was a dazzling display of swordsmanship. His rapier darted from one to the other, parrying, thrusting. The two men retreated before him.

'Follow her, Bart,' Charles cried, still holding both sailors' cutlasses in play. Bart, his arm dripping blood, made his way to the ladder and ascended slowly. The king, moving backward, felt the lowest rung beneath his foot and began to mount, his sword still keeping the two clumsy sailors at a distance. He felt a breeze from the open hatch above.

At the top he looked down at the fierce faces, and deliberately hurled his lantern at them. They tumbled backwards in a heap, and the king was free.

The rest of the crew had been huddled terrified, beneath the rise of the poop. Suddenly one cried, 'It's the king. Let go, fore and aft, or he'll get away!' One sailor leaped to the bows and slashed the cable that held the ship to the wharfside; a second did the same at the stern. *Fancy Anne* quivered and began to drift with the ebb tide.

'Polly, Bart, jump for it!' Charles commanded. The main deck lay only a few feet above the quay, and in a trice all three were picking themselves up from the gravel.

They looked back. The slave ship whirled with the current, out of control. A helmsman leaped to the wheel and tried to head her into the wind. But every second took her farther from land. Now she was ten feet out, now twenty. She hung, teetering as the steersman fought the bucking wheel. But with no way on her, *Fancy Anne* could not respond.

Tongues of fire licked out of the port-holes, and there was a dull roar. The entire deck seemed to lift. A mass of flames shot up, coiling about the masts. The gunpowder kegs, ignited by the lanterns smouldering in the slaves' quarters, had done their work. Explosion followed explosion, as keg after keg caught fire. The masts crumpled and the sails, tearing loose, enveloped the ship in a winding sheet of flame.

Polly, Bart and the king watched horrified, chilled by the sight of the blazing inferno. One sailor leaped into the river. His body fell like a living torch, extinguished when it sank beneath the rippling black river.

Fancy Anne settled by the stern and water poured across what remained of her poop. There was a hiss and a dense cloud of steam, as her white-hot anchor broke loose and plunged beneath the surface. Then her bow reared until the ship seemed to stand on end. It disappeared and *Fancy Anne* was gone.

On the wharf, horses pawed and neighed.

'This way, sire.'

It was Will Chiffinch.

'Well done, Will,' said the king, vaulting into the saddle. Triumphant, but saddened by the carnage he'd left behind, he led the little party through the charred streets of the City, westward towards Whitehall Palace.

CHAPTER XIII

MASQUERS AND BEGGARS

Several yards east of the Holbein Gate, Charles reined in his horse. The others drew up beside him. It was late. Only a few stray revellers drifted through the street. In the palace, candles flickered at a random scattering of windows.

'I feel, Bart,' said the king, 'as a worm must, immediately before it is baited to the hook. Do you go before and warn my guard to take their positions about the privy apartments. But not ostentatiously. There must be no show of force. If so, our friends may not dare to strike and we shall, as my ancestor, Macbeth, remarked, have scotched the snake, not killed it.'

Polly asked, 'Can you trust your men, my liege? May some of them not be in Kinnerton's pay?'

'Never! They are loyal to the last yeoman.'

'Be not so certain, sire,' Bart cautioned.

'And who is to safeguard my person else? Hasten, Bart, and do as I command. I must not be late for my own abduction!'

'Hold, Master Ravenscroft.' The voice came from the shadows. Lord Clarendon's small stooping figure emerged on to the roadway. 'My liege –' He hastened over to the king.

Charles was taken aback: surely Clarendon knew nothing of all this? He asked with some irritation, 'Why up so late, my lord?'

'Sire,' said the ageing courtier earnestly, 'I pray you heed Master Ravenscroft's counsel. You need no guard. Indeed, at this juncture, who among your household is to be trusted? But have no fear. Your Majesty will be staunchly protected none the less.'

'You speak in riddles.' The king looked sharply first at Clarendon, then at Bart. 'Who dared to draw my Lord Clarendon into this imbroglio? And what schemes have you all concocted behind my back? Is not the king to know what the king's subjects do – and that within his own palace?'

His horse pawed the ground impatiently, whinnying. 'Whoa, are you too in revolt against me?' He patted its neck reassuringly, and the horse stood still.

'I beg of you, sire,' Bart pleaded, 'go to your chambers as if everything were normal. Not a hair of your head is in danger.'

Charles eyed him keenly. 'You wish me not to know your plans so that I may not by inadvertence betray them to my enemies. Is that it?'

'Yes, sire.' Ravenscroft was relieved at the king's understanding.

But Charles went on. 'Or that, if privy to them, I might object? Which is it Master Ravenscroft? Which, my Lord of Clarendon?'

Clarendon replied, 'A little of each, Your Majesty.'

'Very well. Then I place my crown and my life in the hands of a boy and an old man. If matters miscarry, may God forgive you both. You have my word for it that I shall not.'

He spurred his animal and cantered off under the gate's arch, past the guards and into the palace. Bart and Polly followed.

Bart held the reins, as the king and the girl dismounted. A groom led the horses away.

'I will say good night now, Poll,' said Charles with an affectionate but weary smile. 'Sleep well. What is to pass next may not be for your eyes. You have, this night, already seen more than enough of bloodshed.'

Polly meditatively surveyed the king and Bart in turn. 'I know not what the coming hours may bring, sire,' she said at last, 'but if you are to retire to your apartments in your wonted way, thus betraying no sign of agitation, might it not look more natural if I –'

Charles chuckled. 'So the king's "natural" way of approaching his bedchamber is with a wench on his arm? Od's fish, what a reputation for a monarch to have! But –' he sought Bart's reassurance, 'what say you? Is the king's wench right? And can we be certain she will come to no harm at the hands of these ruffians?'

'Faith, my lord,' Bart replied, 'she has dispatched one of

your enemies this night already. I am an unseasoned warrior, but I vow I would as lief fight beside Poll as beside Prince Rupert himself!'

'Aye,' Charles replied, 'you're a bonny fighter, girl. Loosen your hair. And, Bart, give her your cloak, to hide the breeches. Then come, Poll, my arm about your slim waist, thus. Your head leaning – so – upon my shoulder.'

Bart felt ill at ease as he walked behind them through the scented darkness of the garden. It was only a charade, of course, but Polly was the woman he loved. His heart lifted when she glanced back at him across the king's powerful shoulder. And winked.

Unseen eyes watched as Charles and Polly, amorously entwined, passed along the corridors. At the entrance to his own quarters, Charles said in a loud clear voice. 'Good night, Master Ravenscroft. May you sleep as sweetly as I intend to do.'

'Good night, sire.'

The king whispered, 'But stray not too far. If you hear anything untoward, come swiftly.' Bart bowed, withdrew, and descended the narrow steps towards the river-gate. There he could hear any disturbance or cry for help, but remain unseen.

Silence hung heavily, broken only by the soft lapping of the Thames as the ebb tide swept by. He thought of *Fancy Anne*'s scorched timbers lying fathoms down upon the river mud. His arm hurt where the cutlass had ripped his flesh, but the blood had dried. He flexed his muscles. The arm would serve; in any case, it was, by good luck, not his sword-arm. He settled down to his vigil.

In his bedchamber, Charles poured Polly a stoup of wine. He raised his goblet to her wooingly. 'I drink to our night, lovely Poll.' Their silver flagons clinked.

All sound was deadened by the heavy tapestries that covered the walls; they showed hunting scenes. In one, horsemen, their spears raised, held a fierce, snarling boar at bay, its tusks bared, its eyes ablaze; in another, a huntsman with bow and arrow, stalked a mountain lion.

Charles bent and kissed Polly's lips. They were cold. Looking beyond the girl's shoulder at the tapestry with the boar it seemed to him that the woven beast's heavy flanks moved; it was as if the cornered creature were panting. The king rubbed his eyes. It must be weariness, Charles thought. The night's exertions had been more trying than he realized.

Then he heard a rustling outside his door, as of stealthy footsteps. This was no idle play of his imagination.

Polly heard it, too, and stiffened. He placed his hand reassuringly on hers. He felt the chill of steel. The poignard Bart had given her, blooded once already, was clutched against her palm, the blade half hidden beneath her sleeve. Charles straightened up, facing the entrance. He eased his rapier in its scabbard. Slowly the door opened. There, with a mocking smile on his lips, stood the Earl of Kinnerton.

The king faced him coldly.

'We have no engagement at this time, I believe, Lord Kinnerton? Or have I forgotten?'

'No engagement, sire. No.'

'Then what possible reason can you give for presenting yourself unannounced, at so unseemly an hour, and when I am occupied in matters of state?'

'Of state?' Kinnerton's eyes turned to Polly. He remained outwardly composed, but a flicker of his eyelids betrayed his consternation. How had the minx enticed Pargiter into freeing her? She could never have escaped *Fancy Anne* without his complicity.

'As you know,' said Charles, breaking into Kinnerton's conjectures, 'Mistress Fitch is one of my advisers. You appear surprised to see her. Had you thought her elsewhere?'

'I had expected to find Your Majesty alone.'

'Well, since you see that I am not, I must beg of you to grant me the privacy of my own chamber!'

'I would not for all the world interfere with Your Majesty's royal duties.' His glance at Polly was an open sneer. 'But you might forgive my lack of ceremonial, if you knew my errand.'

'And that is –?'

'To present to you the masquers.'

'I have summoned no masquers, my lord.'

'No, but the cream of a pleasure is, surely, its unexpectedness.'

'Tomorrow will do quite well enough.'

Kinnerton spoke on, as though the king had not said a word.

'Nay, sire, this masque which I propose to present must be served up as soon as it is ready. Like a good omelette, its texture is destroyed if it is allowed to linger.'

'I have already told you, my lord of Kinnerton, that I am in no mood for mummery!'

'But, as did your royal sire, you have a love for art. And I assure you, Your Majesty, the artistry of my players surpasses anything you have ever seen!'

'My lord,' Charles replied, anger edging his tone, 'must I summon my guard? Or will you be gone in peace?'

'The masque,' Kinnerton's imperturbable voice flowed on, 'is one entitled *Claudius Redivivus*.'

'I command you –'

'Claudius, you recall, was the King of Denmark and the uncle of Hamlet. A lecherous, treacherous monarch – at last dispatched by his brother's son. Will you not meet the players, sire?'

'Leave my chamber this instant, my lord, or you'll play your masque in the Tower of London!'

'In the play, it was Prince Hamlet who avenged the disgrace to the fair state of Denmark. But masques and plays differ, do they not? Come forth, players!'

He stepped aside with the flourish of a showman.

'Behold, Your Majesty, those who would dispose of the new King Claudius!' The weird band of creatures who had been roaming the palace entered. First came the lion, tall and powerfully built; then the jackass, the catamount, a dragon, a griffon, a small stooped fellow wearing the head of a hideous toad, another, tall and lean, clothed all in scales with the face of an adder, open-mouthed, fangs protruding, ready to strike.

One carried several lengths of heavy cord, the others bore daggers or short swords. They dispersed noiselessly about the room until Charles and Polly were surrounded. The king coolly surveyed his outlandish enemies.

'What means this lunacy, Kinnerton?' he asked calmly. 'You have taken leave of your senses. Go at once, and take your rapscallion mummers with you.'

'It were best, my lord king, to accompany us quietly. If you do not, we are prepared to bind you.' He gestured to the cords.

'Quietly? What think you my guards would say to see their sovereign led away – bound or unbound – by such as these?'

'Only,' Kinnerton replied smoothly, 'that one more madcap prank was afoot in the palace of merry King Charles.'

'And if I refuse?'

'Charles!'

A woman's voice, soft but imperious. Catherine of Braganza stood in the open doorway, staring unafraid at the bizarre monsters who menaced her husband.

'Catherine!' The king spoke in sudden agony. 'I sent you to Windsor! What make you in Whitehall?'

'And you truly believed that I would leave with you in danger?'

'Beloved,' Charles's voice was tortured, 'for Christ's sake, go. I, the king, command you!'

'And I, the queen, refuse.'

'Madame,' Polly screamed, 'beware! Behind you!'

The queen swung about. But she was too late. The little toad-man had already seized her arms from behind.

Kinnerton smiled with unabashed satisfaction.

'If you resist us, Your Majesty, the first person to die will not be yourself, but your lady queen.'

'God's wounds,' the king thundered, 'but you shall pay for this treason. I'll not rest until each head in this room is spitted upon a pike above London Bridge! Take your impious hands off Her Majesty!' But the toad-man merely backed towards the tapestried wall, Catherine's arms still firmly in his grip. Charles started towards her.

Polly cried, 'No, sire, no! The thing holds a dagger at her back.'

Catherine's cheeks were chalk-white, but her mouth and chin were firm. 'Heed me not, my love,' she said simply. 'Protect yourself.'

'Seize him,' Kinnerton ordered. The beasts edged forward, tightening their ring. Then an unearthly guttering sob broke from the toad-mask. Its wearer slumped to the floor.

'What ails him?' Kinnerton muttered. He saw at once. The toad-man lay face down, and blood poured from his back.

The tapestry behind him rippled and Whipt Ned stepped forth, a bloody knife in his hand.

'Strike, rogues,' he called. The tapestry was thrown back, and the chamber filled with an army of the king's defenders. But they wore no uniforms, only the rags and tatters of Bandyleg Lane.

'Strike them down, clapperdogeons and rufflers! Lay on for your lord,' roared Ned.

Bart had come running when he heard the fracas. He swung the door open and broke through the mêlée to the king's side, his sword unsheathed. Polly drew Catherine into the protection of the huge four-poster bed near the window.

With a yell of fury the men of Bandyleg Lane attacked. Some carried heavy clubs, some rusty swords, one, a butcher's cleaver.

Charles, Bart and Ned faced Kinnerton, the lion and the catamount. Their swords clashed and the three drove like one man into the very faces of their opponents. The catamount soon fell, clawing at his breast where Bart's sword had buried half its blade. The lean, lithe fellow in the scales and the adder's head leaped to the lion's side.

The huge lion, bearing down hard, struck the king's sword from his hand. At that precise second, one of Ned's men downed the adder, and Charles seized the poignard held in his scaly fist.

Though the fight was unequal, dagger against sword, Charles's great height and powerful body forced the lion back into a corner where he had not the space to wield his rapier. They strained against each other, the sword clattered to the floor and Charles drew his poignard back to deliver a mortal thrust. But the lion slipped suddenly beneath his arm and fled screaming.

By now the beggars were driving the masquers howling

across the chamber and down the corridor beyond.

Bart and Kinnerton duelled alone, the battle moving swiftly from corner to corner. Both were superb swordsmen; but Bart, expertly schooled as he was, had never before until that night aboard *Fancy Anne*, fought for his life. Kinnerton, well-tried in the field, had the edge. Charles joined Bart.

Even confronted by the two, Kinnerton's skill triumphed. He held them off long enough to cover his retreat towards the door. Then with a victorious cry he bounded backwards and out of the room.

Charles started after him, but he was stopped by an urgent cry from Polly.

'Look to the queen, my liege!'

Charles pivoted. Catherine lay crumpled on the floor, scarcely breathing. Swiftly the king bent over her. 'Is she hurt, Polly?' He slipped his arm around the limp shoulders and raised her head, cradling it against his chest. 'My love, my wife, have they wounded you?'

Polly looked down at this eloquent tableau – evidence of a strange but wondrous marriage. *He really loves her*, flashed through her mind.

'Nay, Your Majesty. The queen is not wounded. She has only swooned.'

Discreetly, the girl turned away. Her eyes wandered about the chamber in which her life had been transformed. It was a shambles, the tapestries torn from the walls, delicate furniture overturned and splintered. Several of the masquers lay twitching in death, their macabre animal-heads wagging to and fro as they struggled for a last breath.

She could hear the far-off sound of fighting. Leaving the king alone with his queen, she stepped out into the passage. Charles did not even glance up to see her go. She felt acutely alone.

A few steps away she stumbled over a body. It was Galloping Jack's, lying crumpled in the shaggy coat of the lion. Through his breast was a sword which she recognized: the elegantly-jewelled weapon of the Earl of Kinnerton. The lion's head was gone.

Polly raced along the corridor. Somewhere ahead, running feet echoed. She ran faster. At a turning she caught sight of a lion-headed man crossing a small gallery.

'Hold, my Lord of Kinnerton,' she cried out. 'Throw yourself on the king's mercy. You have no other option.'

Kinnerton hesitated and looked back, peering at her through the slits of the lion's head he had snatched from the man he had murdered. Then he sped on, up a set of steps and out of sight.

Polly looked about her for help but there was none. With Bart's poignard in her hand, she began to run in the direction Kinnerton had taken.

He fled to an upper floor. She followed on through a string of shadowy ornate chambers. Now she was barely twenty yards behind the huge head with its tossing mane. In the very next room, she was certain, she must catch up with him. Yet when she reached it, it was empty.

She stopped, staring about. This was the last room on that floor. No door except the one she'd entered by opened out on any side. There was nowhere for Kinnerton to hide. The walls were wainscoted with heavy oak, in the style of an earlier age. No nooks, no crannies. A few pieces of furniture stood stacked together under dust covers in the centre of the floor. Polly lifted a corner of one cover. Then another. Kinnerton had vanished.

The chamber's windows from one wall looked down on to a tiny garden, and, from the others on to the river, far below. Polly peered over the sills of each in turn. It was impossible for Kinnerton to have climbed down. The drop was a clear seventy feet, and completely bare of ivy. She turned back. If he had not escaped, he must still be within the palace. But where?

Wearily, she slumped against the wall. She heard a slight click, and the panel behind her eased back with the pressure of her weight. A secret door creaked open to reveal a narrow spiral staircase, leading upward.

She climbed quickly, felt a puff of breeze from above and emerged upon the roof, beneath the stars.

163

Only a few yards away, close to the serrated battlement, where it overhung the water, paced a tall slim man wearing a lion's head.

She sensed the finality of their last fatal confrontation. An unwonted authority flooded through her. Only she alone could now speak for the sovereign. Willingly, she took up the challenge.

'Lord Kinnerton, I command you in the king's name to surrender. You must submit yourself to my keeping and to the king's pleasure.'

She began to tremble at her own audacity. The poignard almost slipped from her grip, so wet was her hand with sweat. Kinnerton's voice came, muffled, from within the heavy lion's head.

'Polly, you speak like a fool.'

She responded with quiet, controlled anger: ignorant of court ways she might be, but a fool she was not, of that she was certain.

'Remove that ridiculous object from your head, my lord, and pledge me your word as a gentleman that you will come with me peacefully.' It was not humble Polly Fitch, but the majesty of the Crown and the well-being of the entire people of England that confronted him.

Kinnerton raised both his hands and lifted the beast's head as a knight might remove his helmet. His lean, handsome face was fishbelly-white with fear and anguish. He held the head in one arm, cradled against his side.

'Alas, Polly, you know I could not do as you ask, even if I would. The king would show me no mercy.' He stopped, biting his lip as if in thought. 'Beautiful Polly – for indeed you are beautiful – will you listen to what I wish to say?'

'I have no choice, Lord Kinnerton, but I warn you now, that there is naught you can advance to alter my resolve to deliver you as a prisoner to His Majesty.'

Kinnerton tried to laugh. 'How can you hope to overcome me, if it should come to that? You escaped from the slave ship, how I do not know. Perhaps by outwitting that idiot, Pargiter. But in physical combat, a man must always defeat a woman.'

'I am as tall as you, Lord Kinnerton. And as strong. Perhaps stronger, for I have lived hard and your life has been easy. I have a further advantage – no, two. I am right, and you are wrong. I am armed and you are not.'

'It matters not, Mistress Fitch. I cannot do battle with a woman.'

'Then forget that I am a woman. I am not one of your mincing, soft court ladies.' She was completely calm now. 'Will you come with me?'

Kinnerton sat down in one of the embrasures in the battlement, the lion's head at his feet.

'Polly, there has never been such a woman as you. In better times and other places, we might have met as lovers, not as enemies.'

His dark expressive eyes embraced her – challengingly, lustfully. 'It is not too late for love to tke the place of enmity.'

'Come, my lord, this is but trifling. You insult my intelligence, and degrade what remains of your own dignity.'

He ignored her words and leaned forward, one hand toying with the lion's mane, his warm eyes holding her own. 'Downstream *Fancy Anne* still waits. A skiff hangs on the tide just beyond the steps below us. Come with me and we shall sail together to a new land.

'What say you to Spain? I have estates near Seville where the oranges dangle from the trees like golden globes, and we shall sleep beneath the magically-fashioned ceilings of the Moorish conquerors. A new life, Polly, far from the snow and rain of this wretched island. I have vineyards there, with grapes like topaz jewels. You would live like a queen.

'Or we could venture farther, to a whole new world – to Sicily or Corfu or the islands of Homer's Aegean.'

He rose, his back to the parapet. 'Let us begin again, Polly. Let us be to each other what we might have been had life been set upon a different course.'

His voice was low, vibrant. '*Fancy Anne's* sails are ready to unfurl. The tide sets for the Channel. Lo, even the wind shifts from east to west. All omens favour us!'

Polly felt an astonishing pang of pity. The man was indeed

a traitor, but now he was contending for his life. His vanity blinded him to the hollowness of his appeal. But then, had he not basked, during all his years at court, in flattery for just such empty eloquence?

'Lord Kinnerton,' she said gravely, 'your vessel lies at the river's bottom. Captain Pargiter's corpse and the corpses of all his crew are entombed within her. You have no sailors, you have no ship.'

He rose slowly, still clutching the ludicrous lion's head.

'You are lying! You *must* be lying!'

'I do not lie.'

Her voice was steady, her eyes steadfast. She moved towards him, the poignard glittering in her hand. He mounted the parapet. His body was etched darkly against the star-strewn sky.

'Gone!' He glanced about him at the chimneys, the rooftops. He seemed to be addressing the heavens. 'All, all gone! My ship, my dream, my life!'

He swayed on the narrow foothold. Polly sprang forward. 'Your lordship, give me your hand!'

'No, Polly.' He smiled a strange pallid unearthly smile. 'The masque is over.'

He turned and then, as if blown by a gust of wind, swayed outward and fell. His scream echoed through the night.

Polly ran to the roof's edge and looked down.

The black water had already closed over his body, and there was nothing to show where it had struck except circle upon circle of concentric ripples. In their exact centre floated the upturned lion's head. Its sodden mane streamed across the surface like an exotic water-weed.

CHAPTER XIV

ROYAL BOX

The wintry afternoon was dull. London sprawled beneath heavy pewter-coloured clouds. The first gusts of snow swept across the rooftops, lingering powdery and white, in sheltered corners behind chimney pots and on window sills.

At the Theatre Royal in Bridges Street the damp cobbles were crowded with coaches and sedan chairs. An excited buzz of talk hummed among the gallants in their cloaks and the richly-clad women of the town in their black velvet vizard-masques who jostled through the entrances, and into the auditorium.

Polly's debut as a leading actress had drawn the fashionable town, and, like all fashionable societies, London's during the Restoration was honeycombed with gossip and deeply-relished malice.

'They say,' trilled one pearl-draped vizard to another, as they swept down a narrow aisle that cut through the pit, 'that she comes from somewhere called Bandyleg Lane. Isn't it extraordinary? From the meanest corner of London! Just like Nell Gwyn!'

'Actresses,' said her companion,' are the scum of society and are the next thing to strumpets, after all!'

A handsome rake swaggered by and whispered in her ear, 'If Polly Fitch is a strumpet, what are you, ladies, but the same – save without talent?'

'What impertinence!' she hissed. The pair stared eagerly around, smiling, and flicking their fans in greeting to friends already crowded on the green-covered benches. One looked upwards to the royal box on the left.

'The Black Boy's not here yet.'

They took their seats, still chattering.

'Nay but he'll come. You may depend on that. They say this Polly Fitch has lain with him. 'Twas thus she got her contract to play Viola.'

'The king? Really?'

A gallant joined them. 'Good afternoon, ladies. It was the king, you say, who lay with Fitch? Not so! I have heard 'twas Charles Hart who enjoyed her.'

One of the vizards nodded. 'That seems more like. 'Tis Hart, in the end, who says aye or nay, as to who performs upon these boards.'

'Neither,' interposed another cavalier, shaking the snow from his cloak, 'I have it for a fact. It was Monmouth. She pleasured young Jemmie, and thus came to favour in the theatre.'

Now the auditorium was filling, and Orange Moll's girls pushed their way, laughing and flirting, through the audience with their baskets of fruit. 'China oranges, sir,' their voices rang out gaily, 'China oranges all juicy.' One wriggled her way into a group of men. 'Won't you buy my oranges, fair sirs? Only sixpence.'

'If I might embrace the tree whereon the fruit grew –' a lax-mouthed youth suggested, sliding his arm around the girl. But she slithered away like an eel. 'Nay, sir, would you have me play the whore? I come of decent folk.' Her eyes flashed but there was invitation beneath the long lashes.

From Fops' Corner, at the front, just below the point where the stage's apron reached out into the pit, came the crackle of sharp voices. Two young men glared at each other, flushed with anger, their swords half-drawn. 'By the privates of Venus,' cried one, 'I swear this Fitch girl is no match for our Nell! And I'll back my word with my steel!'

The other, half drunk, swayed, almost falling, his sword, now fully drawn, wobbling feebly.

'Nelly Gwyn for ever!' he shouted. 'You're a base dog, sir. Nelly's musical voice, Nelly's bright eyes.' A third stepped between them, pushing their swords aside. He spoke soothingly. 'Come, lads, damme, who cares for the play, be the actresses never so pretty? Rot me, 'tis my delight to ogle the vizards and show my wit and feel the backsides of the orange girls. A fig for the play!'

A score or more of late arrivals scurried down the aisles, with a draught of cold air following in their wake. Several candles guttered, smoked and went out. A shout arose from a hundred spectators in the pit.

'Snuffer, snuffer!'

The candle-snuffer, an infirm little man, limped from a door at one side of the stage with his long pole, atop which a tiny flame quivered. He reached up, oblivious to the catcalls of the unruly mob, and relighted the candles.

Now celebrities, nobles and wealthy merchants drifted leisurely into the three rising tiers of boxes. The royal box still remained untenanted. For the play to begin before King Charles arrived, was *lèse majesté*, and everyone knew it. Even so, from Fops' Corner a steady clapping began, measured, derisive and nagging. These impudent hand-claps could be the prelude to a riot. To forestall that possibility, the orchestra beneath the stage at once struck up a jovial rustic air, the First Music, first of the three traditional overtures. They would go on to a minuet, and then to the expected coranto.

But the music was muffled, the basses virtually lost and the trebles almost inaudible above the din that now filled the theatre.

In the barnlike tiring-room, only three actresses were readying themselves for the performance; for Shakespeare had written roles for only three in his *Twelfth Night* – an Olivia, a Viola and a Maria. Polly, already wearing the tattered dress in which Viola is cast up from the shipwreck, sat apart from the other two. 'Olivia', small and elegant, and 'Maria', much stouter, older, almost motherly, surveyed her in frank curiosity.

Olivia then turned to her colleague.

'Does this gown still become me?'

The older woman studied her with professional sharpness. 'You'll do. But one of these days Charles Hart must open his purse and buy us all new garments. Alack and alas, I've worn this same skirt since the theatre opened three long years ago.'

She crossed to Polly whose eyes gazed off into the distance, her lips moving soundlessly. 'Worry not, Poll. You'll not forget your lines when the time comes. We none of us do.' She paused. 'Hark, there's the Second Music.' The strains of the minuet came faintly to the tiring-room.

'May I stand beside the stage and watch till I am due to enter?' Polly asked.

'Aye, that you may, just so you remain out of sight. Go, now, and fear not.'

Polly gathered her ragged skirts about her and walked out. Poised though she tried to appear, her heart was pounding.

After the door had closed, Olivia said maliciously, 'What on God's earth has she to fear? She's the king's wench, is she not?'

'Is she?' the other's voice was mild and faintly reproving. 'Well, wench or no, she must still please the playgoers. And stage-fright spares no one, it matters not one whit whose favourite she may be.'

Polly stood in the wings. The curtain was still down. She studied the setting for the palace of the Duke of Illyria, running mentally through her cues: turn here, speak there, walk again here. A boy crossed the stage calling out, 'Third Music, ladies and gentlemen, Third Music!'

The orchestra struck up the coranto and the actors took their places. The duke reclined on a couch, a lute-player sitting at his feet.

Polly shared the tension that was building up within them, as it has for actors since the days of the Greeks. She had an overwhelming desire to escape, to run away into the shabby familiar streets. She was hot, and it was so hard to breathe that she felt that she must surely choke.

A man dressed as a sea captain threw his arm around her shoulder. 'Courage, Poll,' he said. 'You'll do finely today.'

She asked, 'Has the king arrived?' The actor peered through a tiny peep-hole in the curtain. 'He's entering his box this very moment.'

Out in the theatre, there was a stir as Charles's smiling, ironic face appeared between the curtains of the royal box. The entire audience rose, and the din quieted. Lady Castlemaine stood beside him, and behind them both, Bart Ravenscroft. Charles took his chair and pulled it towards the front of the box.

As he did so, the Duke of Monmouth entered the pit and sauntered towards Fops' Corner. Eyes swung away from the king and towards his son. Vizards curtseyed and gallants bowed as he passed. Charles looked on fondly. How handsome the boy was. What a ludicrous notion, he thought, that Jemmie could even remotely have been involved in the Kinnerton plot. Monmouth looked up and bowed to his father. Charles waved affectionately.

The coranto ended. A moment's silence, then the plangency of a lute being plucked. The curtain rose. The stage duke listened dreamily. When the last chords floated away, he seemed gradually to waken from his dream.

If music be the food of love, play on . . .

Bart scarcely heard the familiar words. He was waiting for the second scene – for Polly to appear. So much had happened to lead them all to this moment. He stole a look at the king's strong profile, outlined boldly in the glimmer of candlelight. The king's eyes were on Jemmie below.

Well, Bart reflected, even a king must preserve his illusions. Surely it was the only one that cynical Charles Stuart permitted himself. How foolishly fond is even the wisest man of his first-born son!

He turned back to the stage. The scene was nearing its end. The Duke of Illyria spoke his last line:

Love-thoughts lie rich when canopied with bowers.

The actors exited, and two stage hands pushed on a pair of flats.

In her sea-soaked garments Polly entered. Behind her straggled the captain and the sailors, all those who had escaped from the poetic shipwreck. Her voice, soft and full, penetrated the babble of comments on her statuesque beauty that rose from the pit.

> *What country, friends, is this?*
> *This is Illyria, lady.*

Her eyes, those wondrous dark blue eyes, moved to the king's box. 'Is she looking at me'? Bart wondered, hopefully. But she was not. She was elsewhere, in a wonderland of her own and Shakespeare's making.

> *And what should I do in Illyria?*
> *My brother he is in Elysium.*
> *Perchance he is not drown'd: What think you, sailors?*

Barbara Castlemaine surveyed the girl on the stage with shrewd, feminine calculation. Like one professional assaying another's form, stylish Barbara assayed the bewitching, animal grace of Polly's movements. Thank God, she thought, with a sidelong glance at her royal lover, that she is down there among the players and I, up here with the king! Were the positions reversed, she asked herself, might I easily withstand the competition?

She knew the answer was no. She leaned closer to the king and let her hand rest, as if by accident, upon his muscular thigh. He placed his large, dark palm over it. She turned her fingers upward, and with her nails scrabbled lightly inside the vessel his hand made for hers. His dark eyes were amused. 'No need for that, Babs,' he whispered. 'She is no longer a threat to you.' He darted a glance at Bart. 'Not I, but another is her victim.'

She edged around noiselessly in her chair, to observe young Ravenscroft. He sat leaning forward, utterly hypnotized by Polly. She had advanced with the sea captain to the front of the jutting apron.

> *I prithee . . .*
> *Conceal me what I am, and be my aid*
> *For such disguise as haply shall become*
> *The form of my intent . . .*

The captain led Polly off to one side and out of sight. The setting changed again, now to suggest a room in Olivia's house.

172

Two men, one tall and angular, the other short and fair, stumbled into the light.

> *Sir Toby Belch! how now, Sir Toby Belch!*
> *Sweet Sir Andrew!*
> *Bless you, fair shrew.*

In the royal box, Barbara, possessed of a female demon, heard not a word.

'Did she outdo me, Charles?' she wheedled, 'in bed?'

'Hush, Babs, hush, I command.'

'Nay, but tell me what she did and I'll learn the same to please you. Say, was she slow or quick, gentle or savage? Had she the French techniques? Or was she sluggard, Spanish and maddening to the blood?'

She drove her nails into Charles's palm. He whispered, 'When I get back to the palace, Countess, I'll beat you black and blue.'

She leaned against his shoulder. 'Shall we go now?'

Charles turned away from her and spoke to Bart. 'An actress to the tips of her fingers, Bart.'

'An enchantress.'

'Would you bed her?'

'Aye, my lord.' Bart flushed. 'But wed her first!'

'And what think you the most scintillating new actress in Hart's company will make of a humble courtier, sans rank and title?'

'For that, my lord, I must trust to my wit.'

On the stage, Sir Toby Belch and Sir Andrew Aguecheek danced and pranced fantastically, like clowns.

Let me see thee caper. Ha! higher: ha, ha! excellent!

Again the scene changed. Polly strode on to the stage, now dressed as a man, her lithe body revealed in every line by the breeches and jerkin. Masculine voices murmured in admiration from the pit.

Charles took one look at her, guffawed aloud and nudged Bart. 'Od's fish, Bart, the doxie's wearing my breeches!'

The king's rich laughter rolled through the house. All faces turned to him. Taken off balance, Polly stopped dead, and stared up at the rollicksome monarch. The king rose in his place.

'Say on, Viola! But, by the wounds of Jesu, I'd know you anywhere for a wench!'

Polly warmed to the sudden eruption of mirth that spread from tier to tier of the boxes.

'I do my best, my liege, but not even our bard can change what God willed otherwise!'

The pit rocked, roared, applauded. Laughter swept through the theatre until the entire audience was welded into a unified, spluttering, thigh-slapping volcanic mass of merriment. Someone shouted, 'Hooray for our Poll!' and someone else, 'God save King Charles!'

London, so recently torn apart by suspicion and hatred, by rumours of religious controversy, treachery and foreign espionage, was at one again, a single people adoring their new star, loving their king, even cheering Barbara Castlemaine.

In that wondrous instant there was no power on earth that could have shaken the monarchical fervour of the small sampling of English people who sat enclosed, hot, sweating, laughing, spirited and obscene, in the Theatre Royal, Bridges Street.

Charles raised both his hands. Gradually the mirth abated. He nodded to Polly and the other actors. And the play continued.

Polly swept all before her, confident, her voice growing in strength and melody. When she began that loveliest of Shakespeare's speeches – more an aria than words –

> Make me a willow cabin at your gate,
> And call upon my soul within the house . . .

even Fops' Corner was stilled.

To Charles, the poetry had an added poignancy. He saw in reminiscence, the same Viola, but still uncertain of her magical power, wrapped in the silken robes of the Grand Cham of Tartary, reciting the lines to him alone, as he looked on from his huge bed. And Polly, swept into the passion of creativity by lights, theatre and audience, remembered too.

It was a night of triumph. When the curtain fell, Charles said, 'Come. We'll to the tiring-room.' He flung open the door of the box.

'Ho, Ned, make a way through this throng for me.'

Whipt Ned, his face gleaming as brightly as the scarlet and gold jacket he wore, held his staff, symbol of his new stature as royal guard, with dignified authority. But his vaunted position had not yet eroded, nor ever would, the lustiness of Bandyleg Lane.

'Make way, gentles and ladies,' he bawled, as he pushed an opening through the crowd. 'for the king's most excellent Majesty! Make way now, gallants and elegances, or I'll crack every crown in the place.'

Charles, close behind him, whispered, 'Go softly, Ned.'

Turning to Barbara he said in an undertone. 'He's pure gold, Polly's friend, but he has much to learn.'

Barbara squeezed his arm. It occurred to her unexpectedly that she was still learning too.

In the tiring-room, Polly Fitch, still in the king's stained breeches and leather jerkin, dropped to her knees when Charles entered. But he raised her and kissed her cheek.

'Poll, you have made a wondrous boy, but now it is time to return to your natural sex again. Here is a friend who loves you well.'

'Bart!'

Bart's eyes spoke all that his tongue could not. Charles chuckled to Barbara. 'Our young friend is mute. Come, sir, let your sovereign give you courage. Kneel before me.'

Bart knelt awkwardly among the discarded costumes and tinsel trifles that littered the floor.

'Bartelmy Ravenscroft, for the faith that you have shown me, and to render you worthy of this misgarmented lady, I dub thee knight.' He drew his sword and touched Bart lightly on each shoulder.

'Rise, Sir Bartelmy.' Bart stumbled to his feet, dazed, 'and now speak to her!'

Charles laughed aloud. 'Come, shall I do it for you?' He took Polly in his arms for the last time. 'Mistress Fitch, may I, newly-made knight of his Brittanic Majesty Charles II, beg you to do me the honour to become –'

'Nay, sire, I'll finish it.'

Charles swung Polly into Bart's arms.

Bart picked up the sentence. '– to do me the honour to become Lady Ravenscroft?'

Late that night, Samuel Pepys, in nightshirt and tasselled sleeping-cap, bent over his journal by candlelight, completing the day's entry.

'. . . and thereafter I to the tiring-room, but withdrew on seeing Mistress Fitch in the arms of the new knight, Sir Bartelmy Ravenscroft, with the king looking on, and also my Lady Castlemaine, as they might be a pair of pimps laying a young couple to bed. A most extraordinary sight, but not more extraordinary than the *Viola* of the future Lady Ravenscroft. On my way out of the theatre, I could still hear the words of the clown who sings at the play's end:

> *A great while ago the world begun,*
> *With hey, ho, the wind and the rain;*
> *But that's all one, our play is done,*
> *And we'll strive to please you every day.*

On leaving the theatre, I did encounter one of the orange girls and behind a piece of scenery did feel her breasts and arranged to faire l'amour avec her another day. Thus home to Mrs Pepys betimes. And so to bed.'